# Adam Frankenstein:

## A Collection of Short Stories

### By

### Sheila English

# Mary Shelley's League of Supernatural Hunters:

## Origins of Adam
## Frankenstein's Companion
## The Therapist and the Dead
## Adam Frankenstein, U.S. Marshal

# Mary Shelley's League of Supernatural Hunters:

## Origins of Adam

By

## Sheila English

# Author's Note:

A VERSION OF THIS story was first published in an anthology called Time Out of Darkness and featured Bram Stoker recalling the story Mary Shelley told him about why she started her League of Supernatural Hunters. This version of the story adds in Adam Frankenstein's point of view from time to time and has an alternate ending. If you would like to read the original I've made it available to you for free at www.SheilaEnglish.com.

Some of these names will be familiar to you. Some of them have been changed to accommodate a future series called The Blood Quill Thrillers: A Supernatural Suspense Series. Names like Elijah Van Helsing as opposed to Abraham Van Helsing. So, when you come across names or dates that don't quite fit with what you know about the classics Dracula and Frankenstein, please understand that I've taken great liberties with them to explain Mary Shelley's *League*.

# Dedication

*This story is dedicated to my nephew Anthony Estrella. He loved scary stories and I love him. For you Anth. I miss you.*

# Chapter 1

## Brompton Cemetery
## 1888
## Bram Stoker

THE MAUSOLEUM WAS EMPTY, but not for long. The mystery of its contents revealed to those who could never speak of it. Bram Stoker, once a member of the League of Supernatural Hunters, now a rogue investigator, followed Hannah Courtoy through the graveyard like children playing a game of hide and seek. This was no game, yet Hannah laughed like a young girl, despite she was older than Dracula himself. Victor Dracula, who Bram desperately hoped would appear soon, before murderous Hannah stopped running from him.

"Where are you?" Bram whispered into the night hoping Victor would make it there in time.

"Call for him, Bram," Hannah laughed as she disappeared around the back of the mausoleum. "Perhaps he'll get here in time to save you and Van Helsing."

Another girlish laugh joined with Hannah's, and Bram's blood ran cold. Elizabeth, Hannah's eldest daughter was mad as a hatter and her laugh was unique, even to the insane, as it held an unnatural tone and echoed when there was nothing in known science that would create that echo, at least not here. The other daughter wouldn't be far behind. The three had travelled the earth together for centuries. They'd tried to kill him before. Had killed people he loved. He was just a boy then, innocent and untrained. That was not the case now and as his hand fell naturally to the hilt of his knife, blessed by the Bishop himself, Bram felt his heart race as the heat of revenge, so close, filled his veins.

Writing his novel had done exactly what Bram had hoped. It had eventually drawn Hannah out. It had also cost him all of his friends at the League. Not that they hadn't written of their exploits and sold it as fiction, but Bram had used his real name, the real names of others. He'd given up secrets the League didn't want known. For that transgression he'd been expelled from the League to find allies elsewhere.

He'd lost sight of Eli Van Helsing, but the warlock would be close. They agreed that finding this place was far too easy. It was a trap, but traps are riddles and all Bram had to do now was solve it before Hannah could fulfill her plan. Bram had solved many riddles lately, for Scotland Yard, even ones that had no supernatural ties whatsoever. Desperation was a harsh taskmaster and Bram took most any job these days.

He stopped in front of the mausoleum. The door stood open, a candle from within causing shadows to dance as in some macabre ritual, luring him forward. It was impossible to see inside completely, but it wasn't one of the larger mausoleums and with the light inside he was certain he could tell if someone were moving within.

He was familiar with this particular mausoleum. There was much speculation on it. Brompton Cemetery was typical, but this mausoleum was not. The dark stone was engraved with Egyptian hieroglyphs and the large bronze door was extremely tall. Bram cast a glance in the direction of Hannah's grave. Who actually lay buried in it, a mystery to him. It wasn't her grave that concerned him, but that of Samuel Warner, her lover, purported to be in an unmarked grave near Hannah's. Bram seriously doubted it was Warner's body in that grave. Warner was as insane as his lover. The League had files on him and his rants of a time machine. But, time travel wasn't the craziest thing Bram had heard discussed at the long, involved meetings held by the League. No one really believed Warner. Though the hairs standing up on the back of Bram's neck, the feel of eyes on him from every direction, gave him pause to reflect. Hannah never wasted her time with frivolous stories. She was focused. She was about gaining immortality and being evil, so knowing she'd made a lover of the mortal Warner caused Bram to wish he'd listened closer when Mary Shelley discussed it with the other hunters.

He pushed all thoughts of Mary from his mind. He needed to focus, and thinking of her, and of Washington Irving, fighting over his fate, made his mind disengage from the here and now. He couldn't allow that, so he turned his concentration back to the witch, Hannah.

Lightning struck behind the mausoleum, thoughts of old friends, and old wounds, traded for those of self-preservation. Bram moved to the far side of the mausoleum, eyes darting between the shadows and where he'd last seen Eli. He rounded the corner just as a bright sphere of blue light erupted, blinding him. He closed his eyes tight, opened them wide and repeated the gesture. He'd seen such a light before. Eli would only use that kind of power if he had no other option. The power drained him physically which was not a good idea under the circumstances.

The light grew, then snapped out like someone snuffed out a candle just as Bram caught Eli's silhouette.

A heavy thump came from the same direction. Behind him the crackle of twigs brought him around. The pain at his temple was his only warning. Hannah was the only one powerful enough to fight Eli, but that didn't mean her daughters weren't powerful, or sneaky as Hell. Just before it all went black he heard Elizabeth laughing, and had a fleeting thought of Mary Shelley's encounter with Hannah. That hadn't ended well either.

# Chapter 2

## Dracula at Byron's
## 1816 Day 1
## Mary Shelley's Story

BYRON HAD GONE MAD, or at least we suspected that. He'd always been unsettled, but this, this was far afield of even Byron's usual darkness.

My sister, Claire, loved Byron even though the man would never love her in return. She'd hoped that by introducing Byron to Percy and I, there would be some kind of magical element come from our meeting that would inspire Byron to have deeper feelings for her, as Percy had for me. I tried to talk sense into her, but who am I to judge or advise on matters of the heart?

Byron's doctor reached out to Percy, though it wasn't until we were on the road, now accompanied by Dr. John Polidori, headed to Lake Geneva that the contents of the letter were divulged. Polidori had conveyed that Byron was ill and needed us immediately, but the letter told us something quite different. Trusting Dr. Polidori would be a challenge now that we knew he'd deceived us.

"As the personal physician to Lord Byron," Dr. Polidori began, "what I am about to tell you must remain in the strictest confidence. As Lord Byron himself has requested your presence as well as that of your wife and her sister I have been granted permission to share certain information that will shed light to the necessity of both your confidence and participation."

He produced the note, glanced at Percy who nodded and its contents were revealed.

*Percy,*

*Two full moons have passed since our new neighbor made his fateful visit here. He was more concerned that we not call upon him than that we come to know one another. The man is truly mad, but it was his companion, not a wife, but a woman who seems to control him. The woman is uncommonly beautiful and entirely evil. It wasn't long before they let their true mission be known. My housekeeper first, then my valet, both disappeared, as well as several women in the nearby village. The night my valet went missing I saw the woman the doctor calls Hannah. She had lured the man out into the night using some light that came from her being. I had caught sight of this light as I prepared for bed and watched through a slit in my curtains to ensure I was not seen. She is a witch to be sure. What they are doing with those they take I cannot say, but to add to the horror of it, bodies from fresh graves are missing.*

*Several nights ago a man who calls himself a Count, Victor Dracula, found me at the nearby tavern and convinced me he could help. He is here now and though he seems to know much about the woman, Hannah, he is equally concerned with what her companion is about.*

*Dr. Polidori had come when I told him of the*

*valet. He can tell you more about Victor, as he's spent much time with him scurrying about the graveyard, trying to figure out what they're using the dead for. For now, I ask, no, I beg of you, come here and help me escape from this nightmare. You are the only one I know who might come up with a plausible story that could bring the authorities here without also condemning me to the mad house. Local authorities are too superstitious to do anything, so perhaps you and Mary can convince Scotland Yard to come? Help me, my friend.*

*-B*

It was obvious Dr. Polidori was uncomfortable reading the letter. He sputtered as he read, wiping sweat from his brow, a nervous tick causing his top lip to quiver.

There was no reason for Claire or I to come, especially if danger was afoot. When Percy asked about it the doctor claimed he'd recommended Claire come to soothe Byron. That Byron himself spoke of her. Claire fell into the belief Byron needed her, but I was suspicious. Polidori fidgeted too much for my taste. He wouldn't make eye contact with any of us for any significant amount of time. I never trust someone who won't look me in the eye.

But, Percy and Claire were committed and I was merely the element that held us all together. Claire's sister, Percy's wife, Byron's friend.

The idea that Byron needed Percy's writing talent and imagination, as well as stronger connections that might convince Scotland Yard to come was plausible. Percy assured me he knew of Dr. Polidori, and the man was exactly the kind who'd be Byron's physician. Either way, Percy brought a pistol and that served to calm my nerves just as it served to frighten Claire.

When we stopped for the night Percy and I were able

to discuss the developments in privacy. We both agreed Byron had fallen victim to drugs and alcohol. Speaking of ghoulish grave diggers and glowing witches were not the sign of a man in his right mind. Perhaps Dr. Polidori had even prescribed the drugs and was also partaking in it. That would answer for most of what had transpired thus far. The doctor's twitching and inability to hold eye contact, even some of his ramblings as Percy asked for more details, and the doctor couldn't recall much. It would answer for Byron's strange behavior.

Claire thought Byron was being clever and it was all a game. I couldn't rule it out until we arrived, but that had also crossed my mind. For Byron to inconvenience them all in such a way was just as possible as Byron drinking or taking drugs.

Byron was dark and dangerous, brooding and handsome, talented and taunting. No wonder Claire loves him.


## Day 2

I HATE LONG CARRIAGE rides. I was happy to have it over with, but did not look forward to the madness I was certain would ensue. We dismounted from the carriage and Polidori instructed our driver to bring in our things. There was little light in Byron's home though he expected us. Polidori was distracted the moment we arrived and at one point I would have sworn I heard him whisper, "Yes, master." Though he denied saying anything at all when I asked him what he'd said.

We followed Polidori into the foyer and he asked us to wait there as he went further in, swallowed by shadows. Claire, never one for patience, decided we'd waited quite long enough, but before she could follow Polidori's path Byron stepped out of the shadows, causing Claire to squeak like a mouse.

Byron laughed and it was as though all the worry vanished. A game it was and we'd all fallen for it. At least that's what I thought at first, but as he came closer you couldn't miss how pale he was. He had always been pale, but this was something more translucent and made more markedly so by the dark circles beneath his eyes. Claire embraced him and he was extremely affectionate toward her, which only added to the entire odd scene before me.

"It's so good of you to come." Byron's voice amplified in the foyer, a bit too loud, a bit too cheerful.

Regardless of the fact that he'd specifically asked for Percy's help, it was Claire's attention he sought with his good humor and charm. She, of course, was all bliss and happiness over the change in his attitude toward her. He'd grown cold for a time, but it was as though that had never happened, as though he were courting her with the vigor of a new lover.

"Byron, we've come at your urging," Percy spoke as Byron led us into the parlor. "Give up this game or tell us what's going on. It's as though you've gone mad and taken your doctor with you."

Byron frowned at Percy, not a frown of frustration, but one that caused my blood to run cold. Byron was moody to be sure, but this look was something new, at least to Percy and I. This was anger, a warning. It held for just a moment and then, with sheer will, he wiped it clean and the charm had come back.

"In good time, my friend." He smiled as he sat Claire in a nearby settee. "The only thing longer than your journey is my story." He laughed and it was Byron's laugh, not maniacal, not angry, just Byron. "You should rest, eat, drink!" With that he quickly moved to a cabinet and brought out five glasses and a bottle of cognac. "Drink!" He poured equal amounts into each glass, the fifth set aside for, I surmised, Dr. Polidori.

"Shall we not wait for the doctor to begin this odd merriment?" I asked, looking around for signs of the doctor as a cold breeze blew through an open doorway and chilled my skin.

"Odd merriment?" The new voice was masculine, assertive, yet held a hint of humor to it.

Byron jumped up as the new guest walked in through the doorway I'd been looking at. He was tall, easily the tallest in the room, dark hair and blue eyes, so blue I could tell their color from several steps away. It was as though energy traveled in the air around him and I felt it before he ever took my hand. His lips touched lightly to the back of my hand, but when his eyes raised up to meet mine there was something there. That energy lived in them, burning bright, unnatural. He held my gaze long enough to be impolite, then one side of his mouth raised in a half smile, the light in his eyes changing back to something more, for lack of a better word, human.

"Both beautiful and strong willed." He stood, releasing me, and shook Percy's hand, but his eyes remained on mine. "Delightful. I am Victor…."

"This is Claire, the one I told you about." Byron interrupted the greeting as he pulled Claire from where she was seated and thrust her toward the newcomer.

"Dracula." Victor finished, then turned toward my sister. "Count Dracula. But, please, do call me Victor." He took Claire's hand and repeated the gesture he'd just offered to me. When he looked up at Claire, she gasped, likely seeing the same unnatural event of the eyes. She blushed then and curtsied. "You'll make a lovely bride."

"Bride?" Percy stepped forward, putting himself in front of Claire which I was grateful for. "Is there an announcement I've missed?"

Byron laughed, which seemed cruel to me as he was aware of Claire's feelings for him and her hope of one day being the lady of this house. Claire seemed unaffected though, still held captive by the charming and handsome Victor.

"I only meant that Claire will be a lovely bride one day. I was lead to believe that is her wish, to wed." Victor stepped toward Percy, the strange light showing again, growing stronger, then fading entirely.

Percy took a step back, his hand reaching for Claire and pulling her back with him.

"Forgive me," Victor said and nodded an apology. "My manners are, antiquated I fear. Byron?"

Byron snapped to attention, made introductions in a disjointed manner that caused me to rethink the cognac I'd not tried yet.

"Dinner is ready." Dr. Polidori came, unexpectedly, from a different door and this time I did gasp, grateful it was only that and not a scream.

The strange party moved into the small, but formal dining room where humble, but suitable fare awaited. There were two servers, both young boys, both pale like Byron.

"So, Victor, tell me how you come to know Byron," Percy disrupted the silence. We'd been told, through Byron's note, but Percy was clever to ask Victor for confirmation.

"I'm looking for an old acquaintance who I believe is in this area. I met Byron while at a tavern and he invited me to stay here, which I am grateful for." Victor sat so still I couldn't stop looking at him, though he'd caught me stealing glances twice before the first course had completed. "There've been many misfortunes during my time here. I fear this acquaintance may have something to do with those misfortunes. Byron informed me you had a fertile imagination and keen intelligence. He thought you might be able to help. And of course, now that I see Miss

Claire, I know the real reason he thought to bring you all here."

He smiled at Claire who blushed again. Claire loved the theater, she loved attention, to act, to sing. Now she had attention from two handsome men and the effects were worse than any cognac could be.

"Perhaps, once we're all rested, I can help," Percy said abruptly as he stood and pulled my chair back so I could join him. "But, the ride was long and my wife is tired, as am I. Let us rest for now and we'll speak of this acquaintance of Victor's tomorrow to see what we may do to assist." Percy nodded to Byron, Dr. Polidori and then Victor before looking to Claire who'd not stood yet. "Claire? I see you're tired as well."

"I'm not," she denied. "The meal was invigorating and I'd rather stay up to find out more about this mystery. I'll not sleep a moment wondering what must be happening here."

"I don't think that's a good idea," I added, hoping my voice didn't carry the desperate worry I felt in my heart at the thought of leaving her alone with Byron. "After all it would be highly improper as she has no chaperone."

Byron laughed, "Oh please, Mary, as if you follow convention at all! Don't get me started."

It was not beyond Byron to point out that Percy and I were not legally married yet, but travelled as though we were. There was much to prove his point, but I couldn't let him have his way. Before I could rebut him, Victor joined the conversation.

"I think Claire's sister has a point," he smiled and even I felt the effects of his masculine beauty. "Let them retire for now and tomorrow we'll start anew. Everyone to bed," he commanded.

No doubt it was a command and seats moved away from the table as those still seated stood. Percy squeezed my hand, he frowned as though he was working to solve a puzzle, then it was gone and he turned to me.

"Let's go to bed," he said as though Victor's instructions weren't enough. "We'll start anew tomorrow."

It was odd. Looking at the others in the room it was evident some spell had been cast over them. Why the spell had not worked on me was a mystery. Either I had been singled out or I was immune. It was then that Victor turned a surprised eye to me directly. As he was the one surprised I surmised that he was the one casting the spell. It was my mistake not to hide my immunity from him, and too late I cast my eyes away.

Nothing more was said. Claire followed Percy and I as Dr. Polidori led us upstairs to our rooms.

"You must have an interesting, personal friendship with Byron," I said to the doctor, now intrigued with all the players of this macabre game.

"Why, yes, but why do you ask?" he pointed to Claire's room and we all said goodnight before he turned back to lead us further down the hall.

"You've been his messenger and now you're showing his guests to their rooms. You, yourself are a guest, are you not?"

"I am," he answered simply.

He stopped in front of a door two doors removed from Claire's. He didn't speak further about his relationship with Byron, but opened the door and waved us in.

"Sleep well," he said, "We can all start anew tomorrow."

The door closed and I listened to his receding footsteps before turning to Percy who was already unpacking.

"What do you think?" I asked, curious as to what he made of it all. He'd barely let us finish the last course of our supper before deciding we needed to rest. I imagined he wanted to speak to me in private, before things progressed much further. But, now he acted as though nothing unusual had just happened.

"Think of what?" He removed his night clothes and opened my trunk to help me with my things. I wondered where the staff was that we were left to unpack ourselves.

"Are you mad?" I felt nailed to the floor with the shock of his nonchalance. "What do you think of Byron asking us here under such mysterious circumstances? What do you think of him sending a guest to gather us? What do you think of Victor Dracula who, it appears to me, has some kind of supernatural power to control others' minds. What do you think of it all?"

We stood as statues looking at one another. For Percy to struggle to share an opinion caused the hairs on the back of my neck to stand straight. He grimaced which he seldom did. He shook his head and staggered to the bed rubbing at his temples. My feet flew to him and I sat next to him on the bed, grabbing his hand.

"Mary, I have such a strange pain," he spoke as though he struggled to breathe which only furthered my fear. "It's as though concentrating causes my brain to heat up. I don't know how else to describe it. I'm so sorry, but I must go to bed now. Will you help me?"

I helped him change and got him into bed. Once he closed his eyes and gave in to sleep he appeared peaceful and I was alone. Alone in a house with strangers, oddities and mystery. The need to sleep called to me, but the fear of what was happening fed my body and I paced back and forth across the small room trying to determine whether or not I should dress for bed. When I heard a noise outside the door I was grateful for two things; that I had left on my travel clothes and I knew how to shoot Percy's gun. I grabbed the gun and opened the door.

# Chapter 3

## Imprisoned in a Mausoleum
## 1888
## Bram

H IS LAST MEMORY BEING of Hannah, knowing all she'd done, it was difficult not to panic. Bram pulled on the metal shackles, then looked at Eli who hung in similar fashion next to him, hands above his head, shackles tied to a beam above.

Where was Victor? That was the question. Eli's spell tied Victor to Eli, compelling Victor to save the warlock. Unlike with Eli, Bram knew Victor didn't need to be compelled to save him, they were friends, bound by honor and respect. The three of them bound by a single tragedy, bound tight. If Victor didn't arrive soon Bram feared his immediate future would boil down to torture, death or, if this mausoleum truly was a time machine, being thrown into an unknown time alone and without resources.

"Gentlemen," Hannah's voice rang out as though she were inside the mausoleum with them. He couldn't see behind him, but the voice was definitely coming from in front of him, so it had to be a witch's trick. "So happy you accepted my invitation to join me here tonight. I must admit I am quite disappointed that Victor did not join you. Let's hope he does. For your sake."

Eli had insisted Victor hold back in case Hannah had set a trap. Eli was a powerful warlock with increased abilities since linking to Victor through a spell several months ago. Victor's many attributes didn't make up for his singular fault, that of pride. Eli was often a man of few words, but being quiet wasn't the same as being humble. Bram admired Eli, considered him a friend, but Eli's rage over the loss of his sister Mina had made him careless in ways that could, one day, cost him his life. Bram hoped this day wasn't it.

Bram strained to take in as much as his human eyes could see. Not long ago Victor had given him some of his blood to expedite healing, the effects of which still lingered and gave him acute hearing and sight. If this had happened just a month ago, he'd have increased physical strength as well. He could see through the open door of the mausoleum, but the sky was devoid of stars and the moon's light was dulled by heavy rain. Still, he saw her coming. Elizabeth was ethereal in both beauty and motion. But, when she was in full power one could see it was just a mask and her true face was ghoulish, skin stretched tight over her skull, eyes sunken and black, lips pulled back in a hideous grin exposing teeth that were sharp where they were not rotted out. Her movement was far from human. She staggered forward, and then seemed to skip as though she'd passed through time and came out several steps forward though you never saw it happen. He knew it wasn't tied to the time machine, if this was a time machine, because he'd seen her move like that twice before. Her jerky movements were unsettling and caused his blood to run cold in his veins as she grew near.

Bram recalled the file the League had on Elizabeth. It suggested she was a cannibal. It was reported that Elizabeth's illusion of beauty and youth came at a high price from a dark spell. She had to consume the flesh of the young to keep her façade alive. Bram hoped his thirty-three years on this earth spared him her attention, as well as the fact Elizabeth tended to prefer women, on every level of her evil existence. Eli was not yet forty, but older, making Bram fear if Elizabeth were to devour one of them, it would certainly be the younger of the two.

Bram struggled to recall everything he'd learned during his time on the League of Supernatural Hunters. Witches usually had some talisman tied to their power. Eli tucked his away in his pocket and when Victor attempted to fight the binding spell that linked them, Eli would touch the talisman and Victor would, begrudgingly, comply. Bram already knew a witch's talisman could only be used by the witch who bound the item to their power. Otherwise Bram would fear Hannah's finding it and using it to control Victor. No one knew how Eli had managed to bind the vampire. It was said it couldn't be done, not even with a weak vampire, let alone the most powerful known to the League. Eli had secrets that made him dangerous, but he'd always worked on the side of the League, an ally, so much so the League had admitted him in officially, which was unheard of. Supernaturals weren't always evil, just as humans weren't always good, but they were seldom admitted into the elite hunter's circle.

Bram's heart slammed hard inside his chest when Elizabeth stood at the open doorway, licking her thin lips with a black tongue. The candles within the mausoleum danced as the wind found its way in and the effect cast Elizabeth's face from light to shadow, adding to its horrific presentation.

"Lovely as ever, Elizabeth," Eli called her attention to him, causing Bram to let out the breath he'd been holding. "You'll not get much from either of us. We're too old for you. And of course, the wrong gender."

In a flash Elizabeth was on him, her legs locked around Eli's middle, her arms around his neck, face so close that Bram thought she would kiss him. The black tongue slipped out slowly, lapping at Eli's skin, leaving a wet trail of saliva, thick and yellow, down his face. To Eli's credit he appeared completely unaffected.

Bram's gaze snapped up to Eli's shackles. They were silver. Bram had hoped Eli would be able to fight off Elizabeth, why else call her attention? The silver shackles made it impossible for Eli to use his witch's power.

"Sometimes, a girl must compromise." Elizabeth's voice was seductive, raspy and vile. "Sometimes, a girl is just…hungry." When she smiled, her thin lips stretched so tight that her entire gums, both top and bottom, were exposed.

Bram couldn't take his eyes off of them. The way Elizabeth tightened her legs around him, pulling him closer, mimicking a lover's embrace, a lover's movements, while she spoke of eating Eli's flesh caused bile to build up and threaten to spew out.

Eli's head snapped forward, his mouth grasping Elizabeth's neck. She screamed as Eli pulled away, taking some of her flesh with him. She dropped off of him and landed hard on the stone floor, holding her wound as blood rushed through her fingers. Bram could only imagine his own expression of shock and horror as he watched Eli spit out the hunk of flesh and continue spitting until there was no more of Elizabeth's blood in his mouth. Bram half expected to see fangs, knowing how linked Eli was to Victor, but it was only Eli's own teeth. The idea, however, would have come from Victor.

Hannah was inside picking up her bleeding daughter, the other daughter nowhere in sight. Her mask was down as well, but the spell that held Hannah's youth and beauty together was very different from that of Elizabeth's. Bram couldn't help but think of Mary Shelley each time he saw Hannah with her mask off, in full power. It reminded him that witches were not born immortal, they had to cheat death. Most witches, those more like Eli, lived out a natural life. Their lifespan tended to be longer than your average human, but certainly not by much. Hannah had lived a very long and unnatural life. With her long, black hair, her ivory skin, she appeared no more than twenty or so, but she'd been alive as long as Victor, perhaps even longer. She changed her name often enough that the League, with all of its resources, couldn't go back far enough to know her true origins. She'd been called Hannah since Victor had known her, that much they could confirm.

Hannah examined her daughter's wound, spit on it and watched it heal. She pushed Elizabeth away and Bram felt a strange sense of gratefulness for it. Elizabeth ran out, humiliated and covered in her own blood.

"Come now, Hannah," Eli taunted her, his smile slipping into place to match the tone of his voice. "Did you really think these shackles would keep you safe? Come closer, find out what else I have gained from being bound to a vampire."

She hesitated just long enough for Bram to know she feared what she did not know of Eli and Victor's bond. Bram would have sworn Eli was bluffing, but until a few moments ago he'd have sworn Eli would never bite such a hideous creature.

"I don't think so." Hannah's eyes cut from Eli to Bram and back as she smirked. She moved seductively toward Bram though her gaze remained with Eli. She stopped directly in front of him before giving Bram her full attention. "How about an eye for an eye? Or...," she paused for effect, her smirk widening into a full smile, "...blood for blood?"

Bram felt the talons before he saw them. She raked across his chest digging as though she would take his heart. She pulled back with some effort and shoved the bloody fingers in his face, his own blood dripping from the hideous nails. She put a finger in her mouth, sucked it clean, then another, and another. His head swam, his heart pounded the room spun into a black oblivion.

# Chapter 4

## Death Gives Birth
## 1815
## The Frankenstein Creature

ONFUSION GREETED PAIN AS freezing cold washed over his naked body and the heat of Hell itself flowed through his veins ripping a scream that echoed against the wet stone of a great chamber. The scream grew in volume and intensity, forcing his heart to race near-bursting. Sucking in deep gulps of air stayed the screams and brought the revelation that those repetitive auditory representations of utter horror belonged to him.

Memories flew in front of closed lids, but chained as he was to the moment of his birth he could not capture them. Could not hold them, burn them back into his brain. They melted in the heat of the all-consuming pain.

Primal, instinctual need to survive raced forward as he opened his eyes, flooding his senses all at once. Light pierced through large pupils, forcing them to pinpoints, making it difficult to see beyond into the darkness. A lamp. That basic need to live forced answers from the clouded recollection of memory. Recognition connected with words, then with comprehension.

*Fight or flight. Anger or fear. Kill or be killed. Focus. Think. Consider.*

Burning agony, physical torment ceased as his brain pulled answers from deep within and yelled into his mind, "Be still!"

Throbbing soreness at wrists and ankles communicated quickly that the objects binding him were biting away at flesh as he thrashed against them. Again his mind spoke to him, gentler than before, "Be still."

Trickling water, steam pushing through a small orifice, his breathing fast and shallow, measured with acute awareness as his body instructed him over and over until the training fell into the background, silently moving on its own. A heavy tapping on the stone floor in measured rhythm, the volume increasing until he felt fear settle in his chest, some memory deep inside his brain warning him. "Someone is coming."

The figure leaned down obscuring the bright light of the lamp and throwing the being into silhouette. Its shape, broad of shoulder, muscular, pulled a new thought from the depths of memory, "Man." This time the word left his mind, reached his mouth and came out on a whisper.

"What a beautiful, hideous creature I have brought to life," he said. "My machine of flesh and bone and blood, soulless wanderer, mindless soldier." The man reached out to caress the face of his newly-made creature. "I was once a man," he said, his voice soothing and soft, "But, now I am a god."

"You are no god," a female spoke from just outside the ring of light. "The thing is alive. But, until you can control it, you're merely a gardener tending a vegetable. It is my magic that pushed life into the creature. And it will do my bidding or go back to whatever Hell it was spawned from."

# Chapter 5

## The Vampire and the Witch
## 1816
## Mary Shelley

THE EVENING WOULD BE a night of horrific revelations. I followed the noise down the darkened hall just outside my room. The gun gave me courage, but it would be all the gun was good for.

I found myself in Byron's library where a fire burned bright and hot in the large hearth. His back was to me when I walked in, his concentration given over entirely to the dancing flames.

"You've a strong will, Mary," Victor said as he turned to face me. "May I call you Mary?"

"By all means, let's not let propriety stand in the way of a good mystery."

He gestured to a tall-backed chair covered in red velvet. It was close to him, but sitting there would have me at a disadvantage for a quick escape if that was called for. I declined. He smiled.

"Very well then. I can't charm you. I can't compel you…" He stopped, cocking his head slightly, looking at me as though I were a puzzle then straightened. "I can't seduce you I suppose?"

"No. And you can't frighten me." I made certain to let the light of the fire reflect on the metal of Percy's gun. Either he didn't see it or wasn't concerned about the weapon. I wanted to believe he didn't see it, but only because it helped my courage remain intact.

"I'm afraid you've really left me with few options," he said as he took the chair he'd offered to me. "I admit I'm not certain how you'll react to the terrors I'm forced to put upon you. You're a singular person I think. Either you'll run screaming from the room, perhaps even lose your mind to some extent, or you'll try to find a way to kill me, I suppose. Shall we see which it is?"

"I don't frighten easily. And I've never killed anyone before. Either is possible, though, I think."

He was upon me in an instant. I drew a breath so deep and sharp it pained me. His face was so close to mine I could feel his breath. His once-blue eyes were a ruby-red and held a strange, inhuman light. I stepped back, knowing, with that kind of power, he might snap my neck before I had the gun raised. But, I wasn't going to go without a fight. I brought my arm up to point the gun at him, but his arm snaked around me, pinning my arm to my side and holding me in place as though I were imprisoned by a band of steel.

"I think you'd have killed me," he smiled, drawing my eyes to his mouth full of white teeth, two of which were extremely long and sharp. "If I could be killed.

"What manner of creature are you?" Curiosity warred with terror, my mind telling me to engage him in conversation, make him interested in talking, not biting.

"I am called many things. Undead is the most common. Some call me vampire. I am damned, not demonic. I was a man once, just like your Percy. But now I am something else. A 'creature' as you say. Not alive, but not dead. Kept animated by drinking the blood of the living. Kept strong, with power to control others. Their minds."

He let me go and I was grateful for the low settee behind me. Sitting low I looked up into his face, sharp teeth and glowing eyes in the face of a beautiful demon. Regardless of his assurances, he wasn't demonic. I had nothing else to compare him too. Undead sounded much like a reanimated corpse and fills the mind with thoughts of rotting flesh, but he was lovely to look upon. So I chose 'vampire', though I was unfamiliar with the term as I was unfamiliar with what this creature was.

Thoughts flew through my mind as I struggled to hold on to my sanity. Byron was alive, we were yet unharmed and though I was alone with him, he had not attempted to kill me. Either it was a game, or this thing needed us. Specifically us, for I had no doubt he could compel the minds of most any of the villagers.

"What do you need of us? Why reveal what you are when you obviously can pass as human?"

I was relieved when he stepped away, seeking comfort in the tall-backed chair again. His eyes returned to their previous blue and though he was too far, too much in shadow just beyond the fire, I suspected he'd let his sharp fangs recede as well. The display had had the desired effect. He had frightened me sufficiently to ensure my compliance, at least for now, and he had my undivided attention.

"I have revealed myself to you, my true self, so the story I'm about to impart will be easier for you to accept. You see, there are things far more evil than I out there in your human world. And those things, well, one in particular, a witch named Hannah, is determined to challenge me. I can't have that. And I can't have her exacting her revenge, taking what I would not give her, and endangering my kind over some trivial...lover's spat."

He paused and I soaked in the information. It was difficult to move on from learning there are worse things than him, but he seemed eager to tell his story, so I wished to seem eager to know it. Whatever it took to buy time for escape.

"A lover's spat?"

He laughed and though I was certain he was an expert liar, it sounded sincere. "Leave it to a woman to ask after a lover's spat instead of revenge or evil creatures. Or of the fact that there are creatures such as I in the world. Byron told me I would find you singular." His smile was wide and inviting, but I knew it hid sharp teeth and a willingness to drink human blood. I would not let my guard down. I shrugged in answer.

"Yes, Hannah is a powerful witch, but like all witches, she is mortal. Her life's quest is to discover ways to extend her life or become immortal herself. So, she sought me out in a quest to seduce me and have her make me as I am."

"You can do that? Make someone like you?" I couldn't help myself. The information was shocking. In my mind I could see the annihilation of my own race at the hands of an army of vampires. "Is this possible because she is also damned?"

"Well done! Good question, Mary!" He leaned forward in the chair and the light of the dancing flames softened his features. "I have the power to turn others into what I am and they need not be damned already. In the beginning of my reign they sacrificed virgins to me. Innocents. Some I would turn into what I am so that I would have companions. Some…" he said as he spread his hands apart and shrugged in indifference.

"So you killed innocent women and children? Yet you're not a demon?" My heart stuttered in fear at the thought.

"I told you I am evil, but not a demon. Even humans do evil, some far greater than what I do, yet you still call them men. The hypocrisy of man never ceases to amuse and annoy. But, yes, I killed some of them. Never children." He leaned forward further as though to emphasize his point about the children. Something in the way he denied killing children made me wonder, in that moment, what he had been like as a man. Did he have children?

"But you'd kill women?" An important question for me to ask.

He smiled again as though amused. "Women are scary creatures themselves." He smiled and leaned back. "Cunning creatures. Yet, men are slaves to them. Kill for them. They find themselves unable to master their own baser instincts when it comes to women. Yes, I turned some, spared some, killed some. But, if it helps you remain calm, they never suffered at my hands. And I do not have plans to harm you."

"What are your plans?"

"Allow me to finish my tale?" he asked. I nodded. "Hannah is beautiful, powerful and well versed in all things sexual. I couldn't compel her, which is always vastly interesting to me. There are very few with whom my power of compulsion does not work. She tried very hard to make me fall in love with her and since I was bored and knew it was a game, I played along. When you live as long as I have, you enjoy any unique entertainment that comes your way.

"Unfortunately, she got caught in her own game. I convinced her I loved her and she, in turn, fell in love with me. I think she would have done anything for me at one point. For nearly a year I kept up the ruse, waiting to see if she would continue to ask for immortality. For a time she stopped. I drew her in deeper, showering her with affection and gifts, making her believe she was the most beautiful and worthy woman I'd ever known.

"She was quick to temper and I took a perverse joy in provoking her. So, when she told me she was with child I was happy to impart to her that my kind cannot reproduce. One of her many other lovers was surely the father and I wouldn't touch her while she was with child. She flew into a rage and killed every child in all the villages near my castle." He sat forward again, but his smile had disappeared, replaced with a reflective melancholy. "I had underestimated her. She'd been studying me just as I had been studying her. We fought and I would have killed her had she not been with child. I spared her to spare the babe. But, I brought her low as only a lover can. I revealed that I never loved her. That it had only been a game, one she had started, but I had mastered. I told her none of my kind would grant her immortality. I decreed it and closed the door on that option for her.

"So she promised that I would regret not giving her what she wanted. She swore she would find her immortality elsewhere and then she would spend eternity making me, and my kind, pay. We parted ways, but from time to time I would hear of her trying some new spell, trying to cast a spell on one of my brethren to force him or her to make her immortal. Sometimes I would stop her, sometimes it did not concern me. But, she is powerful and vengeful and after so many children died because I'd underestimated her madness, I swore I'd not let something like that happen again. I kept a watchful eye on her, and then later on her daughter.

"That brings us to why you're here."

His gaze locked with mine and the longer he waited to continue speaking, the harder my heart beat in my chest.

"Is she here?" I asked, making the logical leap from his story. "Hannah, I mean?"

"She is, yes."

"Where is she?" I asked. Oddly, I was more frightened at the thought of this witch being nearby than of the vampire a stone's-throw away. Victor's compulsion didn't work on me, but by his own account he was old and experienced in life. Manipulation was not magic, but it was close.

"She is staying nearby with a man of science who has promised her that he knows the secret of power over death. Byron's place was the best suited for my needs to keep an eye on her. For many days I watched them building some mechanical monstrosity inside the crumbling castle. I listened, undetected, to their plans. I'd thought of leaving when I heard the doctor's plan to reanimate a corpse. It was insane, of course. But, as I have seen all manner of insane things come to life, I remained long enough to see if the idea would work.

"It wasn't until I saw them, with their manservant digging up new graves, that I realized how desperate Hannah had become. They'd been stealing…parts, from dead bodies. I was curious as to why and so, for my own amusement, I revealed myself so that I could question them directly.

"The doctor had a reason for taking the parts he chose. The flesh had to be untouched by wound or disease, appropriate in size to the body they'd chosen. He was brutally brilliant and as insane as Hannah. She'd promised to use her witchcraft to help him in his quest and he, in turn, would use his experiments to help her become immortal."

"I can't imagine the witch was happy to see you." I'd leaned forward myself, a macabre interest in a horrific story.

"Her insanity seems to ebb and flow. She was happy to see me at first. She told me all about her eldest daughter, away in Paris to experience life and gain an education. She let the doctor tell me about their plans, the experiments and how much of it worked in theory.

"I left that first night, finally convinced that the doctor would be able to use science to reanimate a corpse, and to that end, give ever-lasting life to Hannah should the experiment be fruitful. As I contemplated a world with Hannah forever spreading her vile madness and death, as I thought of all of those dead children, so many dead children killed, ripped apart…," he paused, staring into the flames.

"You couldn't let her live," I finished for him. He said nothing for many minutes. As strange as it may seem, he was a hero. He was evil, but he also wanted to stop evil. He had some kind of code, a code that would not allow children to be harmed, a code that would not allow a vile witch to spread her madness into the world of men. I was alarmed, not because I sat in a room with an undead vampire who'd killed countless people, who drank their blood, no, I was alarmed because even without his ability to compel me, I liked him, and that made me question my own sanity.

"I could not," he finally answered. "The next night I planned to kill them both, but as I approached the castle I found I could not pass. She had created some kind of protection spell around the place that even included the nearby graveyard. She had obviously thought things over after I'd left just as I had, and she must have concluded I might come back less, well, enthusiastic about her immortality. As I said, she had studied me.

"She came out and told me she would remove the spell once she was made immortal. She wanted to bargain with me. She would drop her need for revenge against me and my kind, and in return I would have to swear not to attempt to retaliate against her. And then she asked for what I am sure she really wanted. She said their first experiment had been somewhat successful. They had reanimated a corpse, but there had been some complications. The doctor wanted a companion for the creature. But, they wanted someone alive. A woman. Someone who would cooperate with the experiment. Of course the entire thing was insane and no woman in her right mind would agree to such a thing. But, a woman compelled would cooperate.

"If I could supply a willing companion for their creature, she would leave to America when the experiments were complete. What was one woman to me? I'd killed women just to feed. And so I agreed."

"You what?" I stood, forgetting I was speaking to a creature damned to drink human blood and incensed that Victor would agree to such a horrible thing. "You don't need us to find some local girl to damn."

He smiled again, but I was unaffected. "My brave Mary." He stood, walked to the fireplace and leaned against it with one hand, facing the flames, but still speaking to me. "My dilemma is that all the women in this area are easy to compel and what I needed was a woman so strong that even I could not bend her will. I need a woman brave enough to stand against a vile, evil creature such as myself and berate me for my deeds. I need someone willing and able to pass into that castle of death and kill the doctor, his creature and Hannah."

"What? So you asked Byron who might fit that requirement and he gave you me?"

"No, not at all. He told me of a woman who would do anything he asked. A woman who was strong by nature and an actress by profession. My original idea was to use her natural strength, her acting skill and then compel courage into her. But, Byron didn't think we could get her without you." He turned to face me, scrutinizing my every move, every word. "I'd thought to use your sister, but then you showed up and you're even more than what I could have hoped for."

"So, instead of sending my sister to a certain death,

you'd like me to volunteer for it? Knowing what I know now? Why would I do it? It's insane!"

"You'll do it because someone has to stop her. You'll do it because, if you don't, I will be forced to kill everyone in this house."

"You bastard!" Thoughts of Victor as a hero vanished and thoughts of the gun still in my hand replaced them. He'd said he couldn't be killed, but I might be willing to test it if it weren't for the fact that the sound would surely bring everyone into the room and if he didn't die, they might.

"I told you what I am. I've told you what she is. Killing a few humans now to save hundreds later, hundreds from a woman willing to kill children as a way to get revenge, I'll do it. I would hate to as you are a unique woman and there are precious few unique women. But, either I'm evil for killing you and the few in this home, or I'm evil for allowing Hannah to live for all eternity, killing and torturing and spreading her madness throughout time. Or, you can help me, and we stop her and none of your friends and loved ones are harmed."

Tears gathered and I hated it. I hated him. I hated every evil thing. If I survived this I would destroy every creature like him, like Hannah, that I came across. If I survived.

"I suppose you have a plan." A heated tear escaped and his eyes followed it as it made a path down my cheek.

"I do and we'll need to act fast. I am to deliver you tomorrow night. We have much to discuss before then." He walked over to me, placing a hand gently on my shoulder as the other came up to wipe the tear away.

I pulled away, unwilling to let my murderer console me. He nodded as though he'd read my thoughts and stepped back.

"Byron will come to you after your morning meal and

give you all the details you need as well as some items you will take with you. We will meet here again once everyone goes to bed and I will walk you to the castle. For now, go back to your Percy and prepare yourself however you wish."

I understood. I walked away, but recalled he'd not told me one important detail.

"The doctor helping the witch, perhaps we know him? What is his name?"

"He is not from here. Hannah brought him here to escape the scrutiny of the doctor's peers in his own country."

"His name?"

"Frankenstein."

# Chapter 6

## Waking to Horror
## 1888
## Bram

THE DARKNESS MOVED IN and out like the tide bringing with it the sound of crashing waves. Bram heard the sound, then a vision of blood and sand stirred his heart, sending adrenaline through his body. He tried to open his eyes, but they were leaded with fear and memory. Instinctively he knew he wasn't really there. He was not five years old, on holiday with his family until vampires attacked them, leaving him an orphan. He was not lying on the sand crying for his now-sightless mother, her eyes open wide, unblinking as they stared into his face. Blood flowed, slowly making a path like a teardrop from her hairline to her forehead, then angling at the mercy of gravity toward her ear.

"This is a dream. It's not real," Bram mumbled and the sound of his voice jarred him closer to consciousness.

He watched his mother's dead eyes and nearly screamed when his mother's lips moved, words spilling out in Hannah's voice, "Oh yes, Bram. This is real."

In the dream a hand at his shoulder turned him as

he screamed, and he saw the kind face of the woman who saved him from his mother's fate. Mary looked upon him with such sadness and caring he wanted to reach out to her. She shook her head and put her finger to her lips indicating that he needed to be quite.

"Hold on Bram," she said, but it was Van Helsing's voice, "Victor is coming."

"Mary?"

Pain brought his eyes open, his body jerking from the knife that made a shallow cut along his abdomen. Hannah stood before him, knife in hand, smiling, then assessing her work.

While he was unconscious the witch had cut open his shirt, leaving his skin bare. He looked to the knife, which she still held, but loosely.

"Bram?" Eli moved as he spoke.

He looked over to Eli who still hung beside him. Eli's hair hung in his face stuck to it by drying blood. Eli's hair was dark brown, but the blood had turned sections of it black. He'd missed whatever Hannah had done to his warlock friend, but Eli's shirt was cut in similar fashion to his own and even in the dancing candlelight, shadows thrown throughout the inner sanctum of the mausoleum, Bram could see she'd cut him deep. He hoped, for the sake of Eli, that his tie to Victor would heal him quickly. Otherwise Eli wouldn't last much longer. His skin, which was already pale from spending most time outside during the evening hours, was much more so. Eli's brown eyes appeared black in the shadows. But, Bram could see a warning in them as Eli looked at him.

"Mary can't get you out of this. And Victor certainly

won't." Hannah moved and Bram watched her move closer. "Sometimes I forget how closely knit you are to the both of them." She leaned, bending slightly and licked along his bleeding cut in a slow, sensuous motion. She stood, blood smeared across her lips. Her eyes moved up and down his body before looking into his eyes again. "I've never seen a human with such a beautiful body. You're taller than most human men I know." Her hand stroked up his chest, his neck and down his right shoulder. "Very nice," she concluded. "Van Helsing is more muscular, but not as tall, not as broad of shoulder I think. But, he's not human, not really, so I expect him to be lovely to look at. To touch." Her gaze cut to Eli and Bram wondered what had gone on while he was out. Eli remained expressionless, which seemed to amuse her.

"They tell me, Bram, that you were the crown jewel of Mary Shelley's hunters at one time. But, I see you no longer wear the ring of the League. Was there a falling out?" Her voice was sweet and to an untrained ear, sincere.

"Stop playing games, Hannah, you know very well why Bram is no longer in the League. What are you up to?" Eli asked.

"Up to?" she asked, but her attention remained on Bram. "I'm just killing…," she paused for effect, "time, until Victor shows up of course. He may hate you, Van Helsing, but he'd risk his life for Bram. Wouldn't he?" she posed the question to Bram, but Eli answered.

"You continue to ask questions you already have the answers for. Is there nothing about you that's original? Your quest is old, your madness is old, your looks are, well…"

Bram knew it was coming before she moved. He'd learned long ago to feel for the tension that came before a blow. It wasn't magic, it was learned through years of experience. The blade cut deeper this time in almost the same spot as before. Blood poured out, soaking his trousers and leaving a dark stain on the stone floor.

He gasped, controlling the scream that could only serve to excite the insane witch more. He knew from years of being in the League of Supernatural Hunters that screaming only made things worse when you dealt with creatures such as Hannah. Mary had taught him that.

"Hannah! Stop!" Eli screamed at her, calling her attention to him. "He's human, you'll kill him. Do you think Victor will come if Bram is dead and I'm all you have?"

She slowed her breathing, lowering her hand, the knife falling to the floor as though she wasn't sure she could trust herself with it any longer.

"You need to stop provoking me, Van Helsing. You know my temper. It's not safe for anyone." She looked at the wound, frowned and shook her head. "He'll live long enough. Victor can't be too far away now."

She stepped closer to Bram. Despite years of training he flinched when she touched him. Examining the wound her expression changed. Worry caused her smile to disappear.

"Let's hope Victor hurries," she said.

"I'm going to let Victor kill you in whatever way he wishes." Eli whispered.

Hannah frowned, turning toward the warlock she bent down and picked up the knife. Bram knew she didn't really need Van Helsing. He was alive because he'd not told her how he was able to control Victor. She wanted that information, but perhaps not badly enough.

"They asked me to leave," Bram said, struggling to keep his breath even as the pain began to wear on him. She stopped and looked back him. "The League," he explained. He had her attention. "I refused to kill Victor. They gave me an ultimatum."

"How interesting!" She smiled. "You chose a vampire.

The king of all vampires. You chose him over your beloved Mary's group of killers? You know, Victor almost cost Mary her life once. He'd have sacrificed her for his own gain. Yet, you still chose him?"

"I know about Victor and Mary," Bram said, his head starting to swim, sweat beading on his brow.

The look on her face told him she hadn't known this information. He had her attention, the knife loose in her hand once again.

"Did she tell you herself?" she asked.

"In a way, yes," Bram answered, his words beginning to slur. "When she died, she left me her personal effects. Her diary among them."

"The League let you have her diary?" Her curiosity was genuine and Bram knew why. The League was very secretive. Even to the point of questionable actions in order to keep their secrets. They lied, made up identities, blackmailed when necessary and some even assassinated those who threatened to divulge any secrets the League wanted kept hidden.

When Bram only looked at her, her smile widened.

"They don't know." She clapped her hands together and laughed. "Oh I must have it! I had thought to kill you in front of Victor, but I'd let you live if you'll give up the diary."

"The diary has been split into three sections, but not equally. The pages are mixed up to ensure certain information cannot be divulged without the other parts. I only know where one of those sections is." Bram's words slurred, his eyes opening wide, then closing hard again and again as though he were unable to clear them.

"I want that diary," Hannah's voice grew low, nearly a growl. "I've killed hunters before. I know things about the League. How many of you write stories of your escapades and sell them to fund the League? Which of you actually write under your own name, which of you have imposters posing as you? I bet some of that information is in that diary? Maybe not actual names, but how it all works?"

"I told you," Bram began, but lost his train of thought. Blood continued to leak from his wound. He tried to bring his mind back to the conversation. "I only have part of it."

"Liar!" Hannah pushed her fingers into his wound and Bram spiraled into oblivion.

# Chapter 7

## Visions from Victor

## 1816

## Mary Shelley

*Day 3*

I THOUGHT ABOUT RUNNING. Victor was nowhere to be seen. Byron said he'd left for the day and would be back this evening and pressing him for Victor's whereabouts caught Byron's ire and he became sullen and easy to anger. Claire became irritated with me and even Percy began asking me what was wrong with me. Victor controlled them. Even Percy, who didn't seem as easy to manipulate, had fallen victim to the strange and evil magic permeating Byron's home.

I found myself in the library after tea. It wasn't likely that Byron would have a book about vampires or the undead, but I thought I might find some clue left behind from the previous night. I blamed my behavior on a headache which seemed to give relief to the others in my party. They were headed out for a walk before the rains came. When I heard the door close I made my way to the library and began to search. After a quick perusal of

Byron's books I turned my attention to finding out more about Victor.

He had to have his own quarters, but he'd been here in the library sitting in front of the fire. Being undead I wondered if his body was cold. Did his heart beat? If he could bleed, then perhaps he could die? If he fed from humans as he claimed, then perhaps bleeding him out would kill him?

I had so many questions and no answers. I'd looked throughout the library finding nothing, so I set out to search the house. I needed to find out more about Victor before I let him send me to my death. He had to have a weakness. Something I could exploit to save my own life.

It didn't take long to search the house. It was odd that not even the cook remained behind, but by the time I reached the lower quarters I knew I was alone. No one to catch me where I ought not be. No one to hear me scream.

The wine cellar was the last room. It was cool, the air smelling of dirt. I lit the candle that was left just outside the room and walked down the few stairs into the open area. I saw it before I took my final step to the dirt floor. A coffin sat upon a large wooden table. The table had to have been built inside the cellar, it was far too large to get down the narrow staircase. How long had Victor been here at Byron's, I wondered?

My heart hammered until I was certain the sound echoed in the small room. I'd only meant to gather information, so I hadn't thought to bring the gun. A mistake I'd not make again if given another chance. What did this tell me, really? Did sleeping in a coffin confirm he was undead? If I opened the lid would he be in it? Doubtful, I thought, as it was day, a time for business and action. He was, in all likelihood, gone. Something inside the coffin could give me a clue.

Courage borne of the assumption Victor was not here spurred me on and it took surprisingly little effort to push the lid aside. I gasped and he opened his eyes, red and glowing, his face white like death.

He pushed the lid off with such strength it crashed against the wall, breaking several wine bottles. He was out of the coffin and holding me by the throat, my feet dangling, my breath trapped within me.

"Victor!" I managed and wasn't certain he'd heard it.

His eyes focused, faded from the horrific blood red to the blue I thought so lovely when I first laid eyes on him.

"There's a fine line between courage and stupidity, Mary," he said as he released me.

I nearly fell to the ground, but he caught me, held me upright as I gathered myself.

"Why are you in that coffin?" I asked, trying to still my heart.

"Why are you here? Surely not for wine." Looking at me, he narrowed his gaze. "You sought me out?"

"Was I to give over my life without even trying to stop you?"

"I can't blame you for trying, but how did you plan on killing me?" he asked, his eyes scanning the room, perhaps looking for a weapon.

"I didn't plan on killing you," I said, dusting off my skirts even though I didn't think there was dirt there. "I wanted to find out more about you. See if you had weaknesses I might be able to use to my advantage." There was no sense in lying. He was clever and I was a poor liar.

His shoulders relaxed as he signed and smiled.

"I think you may actually survive this night. You're a brave girl. If you're equally as smart we may both get what we need. Of course, your reluctance to carry out your mission and your interest in putting a stop to me is quite a challenge for me."

"For all I know, you're worse than they are. I have only your word that you'll release my family and friends if I do this. You, whose eyes are blood red, who slumbers in a coffin and manipulates the minds of others. I'd have left this place, with all those I care for, if you did not control their minds. I have no choice. I'm a lamb to the slaughter. And I have no doubt I'll know horrors this night that will make me question why I didn't use Percy's gun on myself." I couldn't stop talking. It was gibberish. I'd never kill myself, but I was shaking uncontrollably, tears falling freely.

Victor's featured softened. He placed a hand on my shoulder as though we were old friends. He spoke softly as though he cared for me.

"I do not deny that you will see horrors this night. You may wish you'd taken your life instead of this deal to save your loved ones. You may wish to take it even if you return. Some things, once seen, can never be unseen. You will know there are terrible creatures in your world and the shadows will haunt you all the days of your life." He sighed and his thumb began to caress the pulse at my neck. "You have courage, young Mary. You have reason, intelligence. You lack only two things: The knowledge of how to thwart your enemies and a reason so strong you'd die for it. Beyond saving your loved ones. Beyond saving yourself. Fortunately for you, I can gift you with both."

His movements were fast as lightning. I was in his embrace, his teeth buried in my neck, his arms like steel around me. I wanted to scream, but the terror was stuck in my throat. I could feel him drinking me in, but for how long I could not say. When he released me I sank to the ground. Blood trickled warm down my neck.

He lifted me again, but this time I tried to fight him. I was weak, but I tried. He held me in his arms like a babe this time. I watched him insert a finger in his mouth. It came back bloody and at first I thought it was my blood.

He shushed me as I struggled and he touched my wound. The pain ceased.

He looked down at me, his expression more like a loving parent than a lover. He stroked my cheek.

"I feel the strength in you, Mary. The humanity. If I could cross the witch's threshold I would spare you this. Time has run out and you are my only hope. And as thanks for your bravery and your help I will curse you with knowledge you'll never recover from. I'm a bastard and you are bound to hate me after this. I will give you strength from my blood. And when you drink it, I will show you things. Terrible things. In that moment we will be bound together for all time. I will always know where you are. And you will hate me with passion you never imagined."

Using one hand he pushed the coffin from the table and lay me down. He stood, unbuttoning his shirt. His long fingernail punctured his skin at the side of his throat. The blood pulsed out, coloring his shirt a crimson red. He lifted my head up as he bent down. Pushing my mouth hard against his skin, where I had no choice but to open for him in order to breathe, his blood poured down my throat. I choked at first, he eased up and when the first vision hit me, I drank.

I SAW CARNAGE. BLOOD, pooling in the dirt, in hay, on wooden floors. The eyes of dozens of children stared, unblinking at me and I knew he was showing me what Hannah had done. Letting me know what she was capable of then, and in the future. I will not relay all that I was shown. I cannot bear to live through it again for even a moment. To say I was affected, that I grew to understand why Victor would sacrifice one human woman to keep this from happening again, would be a gross understatement.

Victor was right. I hated him with passion I'd thought only meant for love. I hated that he opened my eyes to such evil. I hated that he'd given me something so vile to fight against that I'd sacrifice, not just myself, but those I loved most, to ensure it never happened again.

That hate burned in my veins, traveling through my heart, my being, my very soul. Not for Victor himself as he thought, but for the fact this kind of evil existed in my world. I'd thought Victor an evil creature, and to some extent I knew that was true, but compared to what I saw of Hannah's murders Victor seemed sane and, once again, heroic.

The vision was too much and I pushed with all my will to turn from it. Immediately I was in another vision. A young boy, dark hair and intense blue eyes hid beneath a bed in a room filled with ancient things. His breathing was fast and shallow, his eyes large as though he needed to take in the entire room from where he lay beneath the bed. I could feel his fear as though it were my own. The door to the room opened, but all I saw was booted feet, soaked in mud, smelling of manure and grass and piss, coming forward. They stopped and we held our breath. He walked around the bed and for a moment we could not see him. We dared not move.

"It's easier if you don't fight, boy." The voice was low and angry.

A gasp, then a scream filled the room as strong, harsh hands grabbed the boy's ankles and pulled him from his hiding place.

I could see above the bed now, as though I were float-ing in the air, an angel witnessing hell below. The man had a large frame, large arms, large fists and struck at the boy over and over before forcing him to turn face-down onto the bed, where a large knee pinned the boy and the man tugged at his trousers. The boy broke free for just a moment, turning around to kick at the man, but with little affect.

The boy's bright blue eyes suddenly connected with my own, shock and shame flashing in an instant before he whispered to me, "You won't want to see this."

I AWOKE, FEELING THE cold dirt on my back. I fought to get to my feet, but the room spun and I only managed to sit up. Victor sat on the table, his feet resting on the floor. His intense gaze made me shudder, not because I knew what he was and what he'd just done to me, but because I recognized that face from the vision.

Epiphanies are born from things we don't know we don't know. I had several as I sat there looking at the vampire before me. I knew there were evil, supernatural beings walking this earth unencumbered by conscience or anyone to stop them. I knew I would do all I could to help Victor stop the witch. I knew if I were successful, I would find a way to hunt down these evil things and stop them at any cost. The final epiphany would prove Victor wrong. He was right that I would never be able to un-see those things. Never be able to un-know them. And part of what I could not un-see was the horror inside those bright blue eyes, Victor's eyes. I did not hate Victor. I did not love him. I did not even really pity him at this point. But, I understood and forgave him. I wondered if anyone had ever offered even that much to the vampire?

"I trust I have your cooperation?" he asked.

Finally I was able to stand and he stood to offer me the seat on the table. I shook my head at his offer. I really needed to lie down, gather my strength, my courage.

"I will do what I can to stop her. To stop them." I took a step, found myself steady and breathed deeply to calm my nerves.

He nodded and I turned to make my way back upstairs. A thought occurred to me and I turned back.

"Is he still alive? The man who harmed you? Did you kill him?" A part of me needed to know there was still justice in the world. The small, young boy who'd been brutalized by the large man so many years ago was now a strong and terrifying creature.

He paused, his brows gathering, his nose flared and I wished I could take the question back. It was out and I needed to know, so I waited for an answer.

"He lives."

The shock of it, or the shock of the injustice of it took me aback.

"Why?"

"He made me what I am. He, too, is vampire. Far stronger than I," he said, holding my gaze in challenge. "And I have no idea where he is." He smiled just a bit and I felt some relief to know he'd at least thought of gaining justice.

"If I survive this thing tonight…" I swallowed hard, gathering my courage, "we find him. And we kill him."

I watched Victor's jaw clench and unclench two, then three times. His breathing quickened, then he forced it to slow all while I watched. His gaze moved over my face, then back to my eyes and he nodded without a word.

# Chapter 8

## Frankenstein's Castle
## 1816
## Mary Shelley

*Later that night.*

WE WALKED IN SILENCE through the dark woods. The damp foliage smelled of rotting leaves and new rain. Everyone else was home, fast asleep and oblivious to the ways all of our lives would change after this.

Victor walked faster than I, as his legs were longer and he didn't tire as I did. Finally he picked me up, ignoring my protests, and carried me another half an hour's walk before setting me down again.

Fire would be my friend this night. Fire and an amulet Victor had stolen from a warlock that would render Hannah helpless should I find a way to get the necklace on her. Victor had given me sticks that a chemist had treated that he said would ignite in an instant if I held it to a flame and I could use that to start a fire in the castle. I had several of those hidden in a secret pocket of my gown.

Once the amulet was on Hannah, the protection spell would come down and Victor would come to help me. I argued that burning down the whole damn place would certainly send Hannah away, but Victor wanted her dead. I did too. I just hoped my life would not be the price.

The trees grew less thick as we moved toward a building with many lights lit in the many windows. We finally came to an open area and I could see the castle was less than a five minute walk away. A carriage waited there, the coachman hunkered over on the seat against the coming cold and rain. The air was charged and my heart beat as though the charge had connected with it somehow. A few drops of rain landed on my face, but it had not begun to pour as I expected it would soon.

The coachman jumped down when he saw us and opened the door of the carriage. The woman was tall with dark hair and dark eyes. She was stunningly beautiful and I knew immediately who it was.

She stopped not far from us and smiled broadly.

"She looks perfect for him!" Her voice conveyed a sincerity that only made me distrust her more.

"You'll keep to your word, Hannah?" Victor asked warily.

"Of course, my love." She smiled even bigger and her eyes cut to me. "Come."

I took a step, but Victor's hand fell upon my shoulder.

"If you cross me, Hannah," he warned, "You will need to live in your circle of protection for the rest of your life. Regardless of how long that might be."

She laughed and held her hand out to me. Victor released me and soon I was helped up into the carriage, to sit across from the most terrifying being I'd ever known of.

Hannah would expect me to be under some compulsion spell. I wouldn't have the luxury of hesitation and knew that could cost me dearly if I forgot that. I sat, demure and quiet as we were jostled up a bumpy road, then over a bridge and onto cobblestone.

Hannah spent the first part of the ride watching Victor until he was no longer in sight, then scrutinizing me. We'd arrived without any conversation exchange.

"You're about to be a bride." Hannah smiled. "I can't wait for you to meet your betrothed." She giggled and insanity rode the sound.

The door opened and the coachman helped first Hannah, then me. I stepped out into the rain, the smell of manure, something dead and fresh rain water filled my nostrils as the sight of the old ruins of a castle filled my eyes. There were more windows than I would expect and only half of those had candles in them. Mostly it was the center part of the castle that had been well lit and the rest fanned out into darkness.

As obedient as a slave, I followed Hannah without a word. The red double doors opened from within and another servant appeared, bowing as Hannah rushed by.

As we approached a wide stone staircase, a man descended into view. He was extremely tall, making Hannah look petite, but he was thin, his skin an unhealthy translucent pale. His once-black hair was mostly white, slicked back with oil from his own sweat. As he met us on the last step the scent of cedar reached me just before the stench of body odor. Whatever he was using to mask his horrid smell had lost the battle to the more pungent one. His face was angular, but not unpleasant to look at. His eyes were dark blue, he had a strong, square jawline and full lips. Everything about him was repulsive, yet his presence, the way he held himself, drew you in. He gave me a cursory glance and then all attention went to Hannah.

"I take it there were no complications in acquiring the girl?" Dr. Frankenstein asked.

"None, just as I predicted. And I long to give her to it. To see her face when she gets a good look at her new husband will be entertaining." She placed a hand on the doctor's cheek. His eyes closed and he sighed deeply before nodding.

"Come, girl," Hannah said and turned from the doctor where I followed her to the darker recesses of the castle.

We came to a hallway and she picked up one of the candles on the mantle of a buffet table. What I'd seen of the place was odd at best. The furniture was eclectic, from different times and places, but even more odd was where some of if was placed. There were so many chairs and tables along the hallways, out of place as well as out of time.

We moved along the hallway to a door at the very end. Hannah produced a key, turned the lock, spared me a glance so I could see her enthusiasm and we entered.

"Now, you need to remove your clothing," Hannah instructed.

The need to rebel was strong and I slid my hand into my pocket, feeling for the talisman Victor gave me. I had nowhere else to hide it and briefly considered putting it into my mouth, though the piece was of a size that I'd not be able to speak again once it was in place. I could only hope the clothes would remain in the room as I slipped off the heavy dress.

"That's enough for now, but clothes won't be necessary later this evening when we're ready for you," she said once I'd let the dress fall to the floor and stepped out of it. I shivered and was grateful for the cold to hide my fear in.

Other than the candle in Hannah's hand, there was only one other lit in the room and it was far back beyond a large canopy bed. The room had once been lovely, but now the various silks and velvets, the tapestries and furnishings, were dismal and smelled of mold. If you looked beyond the tattered threads and molded edges, the scrapes and tears and neglect, you could see what had once been beautiful blues and gold, rich colors and fabrics, heavy leather and beautiful artwork.

In the back, near the candle, I could see the flickering light cast shadows against the wall. A leather chair, filled with a huge being gave life to the shadows as it moved. It did not get up, but rather turned and sat forward. I saw the hands and feet first, large and masculine. Other than his size I had not felt alarmed to be in the room with him. But, then, he stood and moved directly into the light.

My heart hammered hard and my mind screamed so my mouth would not. I was supposed to be compelled, docile, and malleable. I could not run. I could not scream. I could not react in a way that would give Hannah reason to doubt me or search my person.

To my credit I stood and did so quietly as the creature approached us. Metal scraped the floor and as he grew closer he drew up short. The heavy band around his throat halted his movement. Thoughts of the cold, my state of undress and breathing all fled.

His height would call attention to him, but unlike the tall Dr. Frankenstein, this creature was broad of shoulder, muscular and solid. His body took attention from his face, but even if I wanted to see it, it was hidden behind long, black hair, stringy and dirty.

"Look what I have brought you," Hannah pushed me forward.

How I longed to resist. I thought my death would come at the hands of the witch, but looking at the creature I realized I might never have the chance to betray Hannah.

He slowly lifted his head. His eyes were amber, long dark lashes framing them. They held curiosity, sadness and intelligence. They were as lovely as Victor's, shockingly so. As he looked at me I relaxed and took in the rest of him. There were scars everywhere, but only one significant one on his face. It was an incision line that peeked out from behind his neck, running up the right side along his jawline, in front of his ear, following along his hairline at his forehead, then disappearing behind his left ear into his hair. It was as though his face had been peeled back like the cover of a book, then reattached. The face itself was bruised and swollen. The jawline was square, strong, untouched by scars but brushed with bristles from whiskers that appeared in the firelight, brown like his eyebrows and lighter than the hair that obscured his face when he lowered his gaze to the floor.

"You'll have to forgive him," Hannah said as she sat her candle down on a bureau. "The last girl we brought to him wouldn't stop screaming and the beast broke her neck. But, I knew Victor would help you overcome the sight of the thing. Now, we just need to know that what we did with dead men can be done to a live woman and you'll be free to…" she trailed off, but I said nothing. "Well, you'll be given to the creature there as the good doctor has made it his pet of sorts. He wants it to have a mate."

The large creature stood still, head bowed, but his hair had parted just enough and the light danced across his face where I could see his eyes turned up, following Hannah's movements without moving his head. Then they turned to me just before Hannah leaned in between us and obscured my view.

"I'm going to leave you here for now. I suggest you keep a distance from him. Victor went through a lot of trouble to get you and I know you'd not want to disappoint him." She smiled as she stepped back, casting a distrustful glance at the creature and gathering my dress in her arms. "Don't kill this one. She's special." She examined the dress for moment. If she thought to wear it she'd need to have it greatly altered. She glanced at me and shrugged. "You'll need this for later, but if the creature gets ahold of you, or if you lose your nerve and soil yourself, I don't want to be looking for something that fits you later on." With that she turned away.

Her footsteps were light as she retreated. I heard the door close and was grateful she'd left the candle. I waited until I heard her move further down the hall to look back at the large, hulking thing with the cunning eyes.

"Are you going to try and kill me?" I asked, unsure if the thing could speak.

He hesitated for a moment. "No."

Just to be safe, I kept my distance. "Did you really kill a girl?"

"Yes."

He looked up into my eyes, those fathomless orbs of amber shined, moisture reflecting the flickering light. He shook his head, parting his hair and revealing more of his face. I wondered if his swollen and bruised lips were frozen, downturned as they were now, or if he could master them.

"Why did you kill her?"

"Mercy."

I wasn't prepared for that. "Mercy?"

He nodded once, decisively.

"What are you?"

He stepped back into the shadows. "I was once a man."

His voice was low and full of gravel.

"What are you now?" I would have called him 'undead', but he wasn't like Victor. Calling him a 'man' wasn't right either though he was made up of what once was a man, or men.

"A monster."

He sat down in the shadows, but leaned forward.

"What of your soul?" Often it's what a man thinks of his soul that tells you the kind of man he truly is. Whether this creature, made up of the bodies of others, had its own soul I couldn't say.

"Damned."

"Why? It's not your fault you were made any more than it is any man's fault they were born. Are you damned because you killed the girl?" I asked.

I could only see a silhouette, but he'd paused, holding still, perhaps contemplating.

"No. I did not ask to be made." His voice was breathy and quiet. "But, I should not be. I am not of God."

"But, you're a creature who considers God? If you are not of God, then you are damned?" He was as intelligent as his eyes lead me to believe. He knew of God and of the natural way of life. He'd judged himself as damned because he'd not been born as God intended. A conscience?

He nodded.

"The girl? The one you killed. Explain." I took a step toward the fireplace and he leaned back against his chair.

"They did things to her," he said. "Like to me. She screamed and begged for death. So, I killed her."

"If I were able to kill you, would you want to die?" Herein lay the trap I'd set for my cellmate. His answer would determine the fate I felt he deserved, even if I could not give him that fate myself.

"Can't be killed." His voice became quiet again, but sorrow rode the edges like a distant mirage.

"If you could be killed?"

"I would want a final death." His voice grew strong and certain. "But, they've tried. The witch bound me. I cannot be killed." He laughed, if you could call it that. It was more a cough, but the pitch was higher and controlled.

"What's so funny?" I asked.

"Her magic doesn't work on me now. She fears me." If the man in the shadows could voice any happy emotions

I imagine this was it. Hannah feared him.

"Hannah's magic doesn't work on you at all?" This was of great interest.

He shook his head and though I could make it out in the shadows he must have considered the darkness and he spoke. "No. Frankenstein says she cast a spell to help my flesh accept the experiments. But, once the lightning struck and I was alive, her magic wouldn't work."

"Dr. Frankenstein told you this?" I wondered. "Does he realize you understand? That you're intelligent?"

He nodded, but followed the movement with an answer. "Yes."

"I had the feeling Hannah thought you were no more than an animal."

"We don't tell her. Just in case."

"In case of what?" My heart beat for reasons other than fear now.

"Don't trust her."

Dr. Frankenstein was smarter than I had given him credit for. I'd watched him with Hannah and still believed he was in love with her, but something made him not trust her and so he had a secret weapon. And now, so did I.

# Chapter 9

## The Time Has Come
## Midnight
## Mary Shelley

IN THE LIGHT OF day, with time to spare, you weigh out your decisions by playing a variety of scenarios in your head. You consider the outcome, consequences, price and benefits to each scenario, hoping to identify the one that will suit you best. Or at least cost you the least, or cost you something you are willing to pay. I had no such luxury. What I did have is what always served me best; my instinct. The creature hated Hannah, but sharing a common enemy didn't always ensure you'd be allies once that enemy is defeated. But, I'd walked in with a talisman and a slim chance at survival, now I was being lead to a laboratory high up in what appeared at first glance to be an abandoned part of the castle, and I had an ally Hannah's magic wouldn't work on. Someone who hated her with every fiber of his being.

Hannah entered the room to find me sitting on the bed far from the creature. She smiled and called me to follow.

"You stay," she commanded at the shadows. "If you're

good, I'll bring you back a treat." She laughed heartily, her voice echoing against the stone walls, vibrating with madness.

She walked quickly, determined. We followed paths and staircases like rats in a maze and I feared the creature would never find me. But, he had assured me he knew the way, just as he had assured me the locked door would not keep him confined. And I, for my part, found courage to trust him and a way to release him from his shackles with a simple hairpin and a prayer.

He'd not attacked Hannah when she entered the room only because Frankenstein was certain the witch was nearly immortal and without Victor there to ensure she was truly killed, I would have become the target of her vengeance since the creature was immune to her magic.

I hoped the dress would be where ever the experiments would be held. I was to be turned into something immortal, hopefully while keeping my sanity, unlike the last patient. If it worked, they would dress me and hand me over to the creature they were sure would kill me. Or perhaps they thought to monitor me to ensure the experiment was safe for Hannah. Either way, I would need clothes after the procedure, so the dress could be nearby, the talisman still hidden within its folds.

If the creature didn't arrive in time, I prayed he would show me the same mercy as the last victim. Whatever the witch and the mad doctor had in mind, I was certain if they succeeded in their experiment I would never be able to return to my Percy. To my life.

# Chapter 10

## The Stirrings of Soul
## Quarter-past Midnight
## The Frankenstein Creature

THE WOMAN CALLED MARY was unlike the other two women he'd met during his short life. Mary was sane, for one thing. Hannah was cruel and so was her insanity. Mary was courageous. The poor, small female they'd wished to pair him with earlier had gone insane with fear. There was never any reprieve from her screams of horror. There was no reasoning with her. No helping her, with the exception of the one thing she finally asked of him. End her suffering.

As HE ENDED HER life, quick and painless, a single snap of the neck, he was given a gift in that moment. Within him stirred the icy pinprick of guilt. She'd rather die than become what he was. Rather die than spend a single moment as his companion. Though his mind argued that he was not the one to blame, not truly, a dark stain blossomed inside his being casting doubt on mind's logic.

The small woman whose name he never knew rested in his arms, eyes looking upon him, finally seeing him with fear. He stroked her face, wiping at tears still wet on her cheeks.

"Am I to always be a failure as a man?" he whispered to her, burning just behind his eyes causing him to blink hard, pushing away tears. "I could not protect you from them as your friend. But, as the creature, this beastly figure I am to be imprisoned within, as *him* I could protect you in the only way such monsters as I know how."

Standing, he carried her to the bed and gently lay her down, adjusting her so that her head rest on the pillow. Smoothing her hair from her face he sat next to her contemplating the pain her death brought to him.

"If I feel remorse, regret and sorrow, then surely I am not purely evil?" he asked the silent corpse. "What must I feel? What must I do? What must I be, to earn a soul?"

He leaned forward to close her lids, then stopped and leaned away. Without the horror, her eyes were gentle and kind. He adjusted the pillow, propping her in a way that allowed those unseeing eyes to look upon him.

"I am truly mad," he spoke softly to her, and then drew a deep breath, letting it out on a sigh. "I do hope they will not come for you until morning."

He shook his head as though it would clear his mind of the memory. He'd been unable to truly help that girl. But, Mary, she was unlike the other one. She would fight to the end. She wanted to live. She spoke to him as though he were any man. Allies. And though he realized the alliance was born of necessity, she would trust him. She did trust him. Putting her life in his hands, not to end it, but to save it.

WARMTH FLOODED HIS BEING as his heart raced with the knowledge that his participation in the life of another being mattered. He rubbed slowly at his chest as though it would quell the intense beating there. Adrenaline continued to pour into him, bathing him in energy. Tonight he would have revenge, retribution and the glory of being needed.

# Chapter 11

## Vampires and other Monsters
## Just After Midnight
## Mary Shelley

TORCH HUNG OUTSIDE a large, wooden door. The coachman stood there now dressed in clothes I associated with doctors. He nodded and opened the door, then followed us in.

The room was surprisingly large with a single table in the center of it, surrounded by copper coils, machines I did not recognize and a metal table with instruments that turned my blood cold and my resolve weak.

A large hole in the roof over the exam table brought my attention to the fact that the thing was sitting on a lift attached to pulleys on all four sides. Everywhere I turned was another machine, another instrument and chemicals. Tears threatened and it took all my will power to keep them in check. I felt a slight manner of relief when I saw my dress hung on a post near the exam table. I tried to concentrate on that as Hannah lead me to the lift.

"Willington!" she cried out and the coachman appeared with haste. "Remove the rest of her clothing and strap her to the table. I need to prepare."

Watching Hannah approach one of the tables filled with chemicals, fluids and powder, I realized what she was doing: alchemy. Some blend of science and magic was to make Hannah immortal. Hannah likely trusted her own magic, but science, well, who trusted that?

Willington took my hand, calling my attention back to my current problem. I pulled away without thought and immediately regretted it. He eyed me with suspicion, his thick, dark brows touching as he frowned. I stepped up onto the lift and he followed without remark. I walked across to where my dress hung, but the man pulled me back before I could reach it.

"Where do you think you're going?" he asked. I felt eyes on me as soon as he spoke.

"My clothes are here. You were leading me in this direction, so I assumed you want all of my clothes in one place." Logical, simple deduction, but Willington looked over his shoulder for a moment and I held my breath. I aimed my eyes toward the floor and bent my head slightly, waiting to be told what to do.

Willington must have gotten some signal since he turned around and said with great authority, with a voice only the weak use when they have someone to champion them, "Alright, then. You may put the rest of your clothes there."

Stepping down from the lift and taking two steps toward the place where my dress hung put me out of the direct light making it harder to see me, but easier for me to see those in the light. Hannah was busy at the table and the doctor, whom I'd not seen yet, was directly across from me working on a machine that was hooked up to the exam table.

His back was to me at first, but when he turned to check a coil, or secure something to wires wrapped around the ropes, I could make out that he wore goggles over his eyes. It seemed odd to me at first, but then he pulled a lever and electricity moved like lightning up the coils and beyond into the night sky. The sound caused me to let out a stifled scream, but no one seemed to hear me. The doctor moved the lever and it all stopped. Willington didn't seem sure of the sound or the light either, and his attention was on the doctor as he seemed to wait without breathing for the lever to go down again.

I seized my opportunity. The dress hung in a manner that allowed me to find the pocket easily. My heart soared with hope as my fingers touched it and I pulled it out. Hannah hadn't found it. I doubted she even looked. I was a mere mortal woman, no threat to her.

I didn't have time to put the dress on, but I had no intention of disrobing further. I did, however, plan on fighting to the death if they tried to force me on that table.

The doctor threw down the lever just as I moved around the outskirts of the room toward Hannah. The talisman had to be on her person for it to stop her magic long enough to let Victor in. I was close enough to fear she'd hear my heart even through the loud noise of the doctor's machine. Only a few paces more and I would have her within reach.

The large wooden door burst open with such violence it shattered at its hinges. The creature stood there looking around the room. As his eyes found Hannah I threw the talisman around her neck where it hung like a pendant, swinging with the force of her movement. She turned to look at me, then looked down at the talisman, but the creature was upon her, picking her up and throwing her toward Frankenstein who reached out as though to catch her. They both landed in a heap, the machine's noise continuing to rage, electric current running up into the night.

Frankenstein was swift and self-preservation had him pushing Hannah off of him while she struggled to dislodge herself from her own skirts. The doctor grabbed a metal rod, with a gloved hand, at the base where there was a handle. Electric current arced from it to the nearby coil. Willington was there suddenly with another, similar rod, handing it to the doctor. The arc moved back and forth between the two rods and the creature stepped back.

Hannah leveraged herself up and pulled the talisman hard. It broke and she threw it at me. Her face shifted, lips pulling back in a grotesque smile that showed teeth, gums and a black tongue as it licked over taught lips. Her eyes turned red and glowed as though fire lived in them. She began walking toward me, not rushed, as though she wanted to make sure I knew what was coming.

I looked toward the creature, but he seemed terrified of the rods Frankenstein wielded and he was backing away as Frankenstein moved forward.

"Help!" I screamed as loud as I could, not sure anyone could hear me over the noise. But, he did. He glanced over his shoulder, taking in Hannah approaching me.

He glanced again at Frankenstein, but turned toward me. A few steps in my direction and he cried out in pain as electricity was forced through his body. He may not be able to be killed, but the look on his face told me he could certainly feel pain. He screamed out again, but kept moving toward me. Hannah caught sight of him and looked toward her lover for help.

The noise began to echo in my head, the adrenaline pumping so fast the room spun. I moved toward the creature, the only ally I had, but how would I free him to save me?

I reached out for him as he stepped away from the rods. I thought I heard him call my name, but his lips didn't move. From my peripheral I saw Hannah look back toward the door. As I saw Victor enter, followed closely by Percy, the creature grabbed my hand and the doctor touched the rod to him again.

The electric current would not kill the creature, but the pain that ran through my body told me that it could, and would, kill me. I screamed as I was hurled through the air landing on the hard, cold stone floor, my breath stolen from the impact.

As I struggled to force my lungs to function, my eyes sought the only thing in the world that mattered; Percy. He was trying to move through the chaos to reach me. Willington went at him with a scalpel and they began to fight. I pulled in air as Percy pushed the sharp knife deep into Willington's throat while that man still held the scalpel in his hand.

The pain subsided and I was breathing again. Percy reached me, pulling me up and wrapping his arms around me. I buried my face in his chest and sobbed like a child. The noise abruptly stopped and I peered over Percy's shoulder. Dr. Frankenstein lay on the stone floor, neck broken, eyes fixed. Willington shared that fate in a puddle of blood close-by. But, when I saw Victor fighting the creature I was propelled up and began screaming.

"Victor! No!" I tried to move toward them as their fighting continued to destroy the laboratory, but Percy wouldn't release me. "No! Victor! He's our ally! He helped me!" But, Victor didn't hear, or didn't want to hear. So I turned to Percy, "He's fighting the wrong monster! Where's Hannah?" I'd scanned the entire room and the witch was nowhere in sight.

Percy's brows turned down and he looked back to the creature and Victor. "Stay here, Mary." He said, then for good measure added, "I mean it!"

Percy moved closer and then ran head first into Victor. The vampire was so intent on the creature he didn't see Percy coming and he was knocked off balance. Victor was up immediately, but Percy had placed himself between Victor and the creature, hands held out as though that could stop them from approaching each other.

"Stop, Victor!" Percy yelled, looking back at the creature as well. "Hannah is gone! You're fighting the wrong man."

Only the sound of breathing, fast and heavy, filled the room. Every muscle in my body ached, but I began to move forward when Percy nodded in my direction.

"Victor, this man helped us. He tried to save me." Now I had his attention.

"That's not how it looked to me." Victor sounded perfectly poised as though he hadn't just been fighting. He was disheveled, but his breathing was normal.

"Be that as it may, he was trying to help me. We had a plan to kill Hannah. Her power doesn't work on him. Now, she's escaped."

Victor was there and then he wasn't. He moved so fast I wasn't sure if he'd left by the door or the gaping hole in the ceiling. Percy, Frankenstein's creature and I stood in the hellish chamber for just a few more moments before I couldn't stand it any longer and walked out, hoping they would follow.

I wasn't sure if I walked in the right direction or not, but I had to get as far from that lab as I could. Percy caught up with me, my dress tucked under his arm. I stopped and he helped me put it on. Funny thing about clothes, they can make you feel things about yourself. I put on the dress and I turned from victim to woman. Though the fighting was behind me, I felt stronger, more courageous, wrapped in the civility and normality of my clothes.

The creature came up behind and nodded in the direction of a staircase. We followed him. He seemed to labor in his movements and by the time we reached the bottom the large man had to stop and rest at one of the chairs along the hall. When he was ready to move he stood, putting his hand on top of a sturdy table nearby, he held there a moment, then turned and walked further down the hall. He repeated this again and again until I realized why the furniture was arranged thus.

"Are you in pain?" I asked as he sat down in the hall that I recognized, looking at the room at the end, his room.

He shook his head. "It's not the pain, it's the dizziness. My brain hasn't completely accepted this body I think. It's as though the puzzle is put together, but the picture isn't quite clear."

In that moment my heart broke for this unfortunate soul. He was immortal. He thought himself a monster and he looked the part. He was in pain, suffering and that might follow him for all time. I could only hope that, one day, science would be able to help him, or he'd find a witch with magic that could. Or, he'd find a way to die.

"What will you do now?" I couldn't help but ask. I had it in my mind to ask him to come with us. He had tried to save me. He had a conscience. He needed help. Whatever followed, be damned. We would find a way to take him in.

"The doctor is dead," he said as he started to stand and then thought better of it. "Now, Hannah must be stopped. She'll look for another scientist. I can't let that happen."

"You could come with us. Until you feel better," I offered, but he was already shaking his head.

"The best medicine, the best treatment, for me is to have purpose. I need to have purpose. I need something that proves I am not a monster. Something that shows my humanity is still within my grasp. Perhaps I can earn a soul." The last words softly spoken caused tears to gather in my eyes and I took his hand, so large and scarred.

"It was others who made your body. It will be you

who makes your soul. Men born of the womb can become monsters. Why can't you, created to be a monster, become a man of honor?"

He squeezed my hand lightly, his swollen lips moving into what I would call a smile. For a split second I could see him through those bruises and swelling and he was no longer a monster, but a man, handsome regardless of his scars, or perhaps because of them.

Victor walked into the hall and we all turned, waiting to hear of Hannah.

"Bloody Hell, the witch is nowhere to be found. I lost track of her, but she's headed east. I'll gather my things tonight and set out after her. It never takes long before her nature brings attention somewhere."

"I wish to go. I want her dead, perhaps even more so than you," the creature said.

"You'll slow me down. I can't wait for you. But, if we cross paths I will count you an ally and whatever I know of Hannah, I will share. As long as she ends up dead, I don't care who does the deed," Victor said.

"What of us?" Percy demanded. "How will we ever go back to our lives now that we know of the monsters in the darkness?"

"Just as I told you when I woke you to join me," Victor said. "Your greatest strength is your love and willingness to do anything to keep each other alive. I knew if I brought you, she would fight harder. And that you would find it in you to kill if that's what was needed. And it was. And you did."

"You're such a bastard," I said to him, my blood heated with fury. "You brought my husband to help ensure your success? He could have been killed!"

"But, he wasn't. And now you both know what must be done should you find the monsters have invaded your world. Besides, you made a promise to me and I think I'll take you up on it." Victor alluded to my promise to help kill the man who abused him, turned him into the demon he was now. "And, now you have Percy to help us. Now that he knows everything."

It was a double-edged sword. I wanted Percy to know and to help me, but I wanted him safe, I wanted him ignorant of the horrors I'd stumbled upon. Victor knew it and he removed my guilt by being the one to enlighten Percy, instead of me.

"I'll put everything right before I leave Byron's, but I need to leave before dawn, so I will bid you farewell. I will leave you my carriage. It's right outside the doors to the castle." Victor bowed slightly.

"But, what of my promise to you? How will I find you?" I asked.

"I will find you," he assured me. "When the time is right, I will find you."

He turned and walked down the hall, turning the corner, out of sight for now. Percy put his arm around me and for the first time I realized I was shaking.

"It's time to go," Percy said and I nodded.

"Thank you," I began, but then realized I had no idea what the creature's name was. "What do I call you?"

"I can't be who I once was. I am made from many. I have no name," he said, then cocked his head, the corners of his mouth curving upward as much as they could. "Why don't you give me a name?"

Looking at him in the dark, dismal castle, I was struck with the importance of naming him. It was his start, a new life. I knew immediately what his name would be and I leaned down to place a soft, sisterly, kiss on his brow.

"Adam." I smiled and looked into his face. "You are the first man God gave life to in *this* manner, for I assure you, no life happens without the will of God."

"Adam," he repeated it, trying it out with that low,

baritone voice. He nodded and stood, holding still for a moment as his dizziness melted away. He shook Percy's hand, then took mine and pressed it to his lips.

It was the last time I would see Adam, though I would hear of him from time to time as people reported him to the group of supernatural hunters I created. His appearance inspired fear for many and he was reported to be in the vicinity of supernatural events, but I knew he'd become a hunter in his own right. Victor had run into him a few times and of course I saw Victor many times since then. Adam was alone in the world, but he found purpose, and I hoped; a soul.

Percy and I found others who had run into supernatural beings or events and they joined our league of supernatural hunters. We grew strong, found our way, became well-funded through those who asked us for help, and through writing of our exploits and selling it as fiction. That was Percy's idea and it worked well for us on many levels.

My adventures have cost me much, but they have given me much. I leave my diaries to Bram, the son of my heart. My greatest joy and most valiant warrior.

# CHAPTER 12

## THE HORROR OF BEGINNINGS
## 1888 - 2017

E CAME AWAKE IN darkness. The cold, wet stones penetrated his clothing, he shivered. He grabbed the wound he was certain Hannah tore open, but though raw and still wet with blood, it was healing. He sat up, trying to force his eyes to become accustomed to the darkness.

"Eli?" Bram called out. Bram was breathing, so perhaps Eli was too. The absence of pain hinted at the absence of Hannah.

"Take it easy. You've lost a deal of blood." Eli's voice came from his left and he turned in that direction, finally able to see movement, though only that.

"You can thank me for saving you by figuring out how to get the hell out of this mausoleum." Victor's voice rang out from the right. The vampire moved through the darkness, part of it.

Bram stood, though he had no idea what to do next since he couldn't see a bloody thing. He felt someone next to him and turned in Victor's direction.

"What happened?" he asked his friend.

Bram wavered and Victor put his hand on his shoulder

to steady him.

"You and Van Helsing didn't wait as I instructed and Hannah captured you. She used you as bait and now we're all here in this God forsaken mausoleum, held prisoner by stone and magic it seems." Victor sighed loudly, frustration echoing in the sound.

Victor applied pressure to Bram's shoulder and guided him to a wall where a stone bench waited for him. Once seated onto the bench, Victor released him.

"I've been trying to solve the puzzle of the magic Hannah used," Eli said from across the small room. "It's been perhaps a day and I've found nothing to help us escape."

"A day?" Bram let the thought of it sink in as his brain started filling in answers. The only way for him to heal so fast is for Victor to give him blood. He must have been near death because, normally, he'd feel invigorated after receiving vampire blood, but currently he felt more like he had a hangover and lost a bar fight.

"Yes," Eli continued. "Victor fell victim to Hannah's tricks and in his earnest attempt to save you, he was entombed here with us in the mausoleum. I presume, just as Hannah planned."

"I'd not have fallen victim to anything if the two of you had stayed put," Victor's voice ground out.

A noise stopped any further conversation. Where the sound came from was difficult to pinpoint. It was everywhere. Stone scraping stone, echoing as though it was far away. Bram's sight had adjusted and he could make out where Eli and Victor stood. Both looked in all direction just as he was doing.

"Do you think someone is trying to get in? Perhaps save us?" Eli asked. "The League perhaps?"

Bram leaned back against the stones and immediately stood when he felt it vibrating. He reached out to touch it with his hand just as the noise stopped and silence filled the room.

"I doubt it. We're not exactly on their ally list," Bram said.

When no one responded he turned, but whether or not they were there he couldn't say as his hand moved through the stone as though it were made of air and he fell to the ground beyond, blinded by the falling sun.

Regardless of Victor's blood and the expedited healing process, falling hurt like hell. Bram curled into a ball, tucking his head under his arm to protect his eyes, though the sun was setting quickly, shadows crawling over him as he lay there. He peeked up, the pain fading as his eyes adjusted. With a deep breath, he pushed himself up.

Pounding on the stone walls of the museum Bram circled the building. The metal door was secure and no amount of pounding on it returned signs of life within. The mausoleum appeared altered somehow and he stepped back to take in his surroundings.

"This isn't right," he whispered aloud.

It was a graveyard full of dead and their final homes. Daylight relieved his mind of ghosts and ghouls, but something was amiss about this place. Once again he gingerly touched the stones, but they were solid. Again he systematically went around all four walls looking for stones that allowed his hand to penetrate within. Stepping back he saw he'd left bloody handprints scattered where he'd first got out. He looked at his hand now dry and dirty.

"Blood? Is that how it works?" He searched himself for a knife, but of course Hannah had removed all weapons from his person. If that were the answer then why didn't he or Eli fall through the floor of the damned place as they certainly had bled from any number of wounds inflicted upon them. Magic was certainly involved.

As the sun gave way to a darkened dusk and stars peeked early in the sky, a sound from nearby brought

Bram to attention and he hugged his back to the stone wall, trying to stay hidden from whoever was coming around the corner.

"Hey, you!"

Someone called out and Bram turned, ready to fight. An older gentleman, dressed in a manner not quite familiar, but obviously for work, walked toward him.

"Groundskeeper?" Bram guessed aloud.

The man slowed down as though having second thoughts about getting too close.

"The tours haven't started yet. Are you an actor? Or looking for one of those costume parties? Are you okay?" the man spoke in a kind voice, not taken aback by Bram's disheveled look, but taking in the dried blood finally.

"It seems that I've been injured. I fell. Can you tell me where I am?" Bram put his hands out to show the groundskeeper he meant no harm.

"I think you better come with me and I'll get you to someone who can help," he offered. "Wait here and I'll get my cart."

He left for a moment and Bram considered hiding, but to what purpose? He needed time and energy to solve this. He needed to secure his own safety in order to assist his friends.

The sound of a machine caught his attention. An automobile, small and open, came toward him, the groundskeeper behind the wheel. He stopped beside Bram and waited.

"Come on. You look like you're gonna fall over any time now. Let's get you to someone who can help you." He patted the seat next to him and Bram took the seat, holding on to a metal handle as they began moving forward at an alarming rate.

Bram cast a last glance over his shoulder, wondering what Eli and Victor were doing. If they were inside that mausoleum, just unable to communicate to him. He'd have to come back late at night and try to get inside through its locked door.

They pulled up next to a small building and the groundskeeper got out.

"You can come inside and call someone to come get you, eh?"

He motioned, Bram followed. The man sat him down in comfortable chair that reclined with the pull of a handle at its side. He was given a strange bottle, filled with cold water, which he drank completely and immediately. But, when the older gentleman pointed a device at a small box in front of him Bram was mesmerized. What kind of magic could fit moving pictures in a box such as this was both frightening and fascinating.

"I'll leave on the news, unless you don't want that? The phone's over there." He pointed in the direction of a small side table.

Bram couldn't speak, dared not speak, and eventually the man walked away. He recalled the last time he was so dumbstruck, so lost. Mary Shelley was reported in the papers as dead, but she stood there offering him her hand, real as anyone. Of course he was too young to know who she was at that time, he'd learn about her in the years that came after. He started a new life that day, born of horror and blood, thrown into a world of intrigue and secret wars. It changed him. She had changed him. She had taught him to accept what was and deal with it. It was a valuable lesson, one he called upon now as he watched the moving pictures with their scrolling words telling him he was in a different place. A different time. There were still wars and monsters, of that he was certain. Regardless of what the men or women reported, he could tell the difference between a serial killer and a rogue vampire gone mad.

His heart pounded in his aching head, wounds not quite healed throbbed with that beat. He worked to wrap his mind around what he must accept. The year is 2017. He was in America, New Orleans, Louisiana. There were monsters to stop and friends to save. He had once been the crown jewel of The League of Supernatural Hunters. The crown was tarnished, but he was a hunter still.

# Chapter 13

## A Purpose
## 2017
## Adam Frankenstein

Cairo, Egypt has changed much over the years, but it was still a beautiful and dangerous place. Smoke choked the city until its inhabitants became immune to it.

Standing on the Kasr El-Nil bridge in the dead of night, Adam allowed himself to enjoy the cooler temperature while no longer acknowledging the open stares by those still meandering around the bridge. Leaning against the metal rail, looking into the Nile River, he waited. A serial rapist had gained celebrity when he pushed his way into the car of a celebrity, raped and killed her, leaving her body in her parked car near the bridge when he was finished with her. The man had spent nearly a year attacking women as they drove around the traffic circle in the center of Tahrir Square, slowing enough during peak traffic for him to open a door and get in. Until the rape and murder of a famous woman, it was largely under-reported by the media. But, Adam wasn't waiting for that man. Once the famous Tahrir Square Killer killed a woman, resulting in an outcry the authorities could not ignore, he'd been quickly apprehended. Much media coverage was given to his apprehension and people waited to hear of the final justice of his sentence.

The man allegedly escaped custody. Unfortunately, he did so while Adam was in the city. So, that particular problem was eradicated, like vermin. But, the man, horrified and willing to do or say anything to save his life, shared with Adam how exactly he had escaped justice. His cousin was Deputy Minister of Special Police. A man in charge of police transport. Youssef Bazzi was a powerful man who'd done little to stop the rapes that had plagued his city for nearly a year, then took credit for the apprehension of the killer before arranging for his cousin to escape police custody once people thought the man was headed for justice.

Adam waited at the bridge because Youssef would meet with a high-end madam near here where a young man would be transferred to Youssef's car for an hour or so and then returned. Every Friday, a different young man.

Adam looked at his watch, pushed away from the rail and began the long walk to the other side of the bridge. The madam would not show this evening. That had been arranged earlier in the day.

Looking out at the great and ancient Nile River he was struck by melancholy. The river was vast and seemed to flow into eternity. With the exception of Victor Dracula, Adam once had only things, items, objects and nature's own immortals like the wondrous Nile River as constant companions. The melancholy was fleeting and he looked over his shoulder, whistled and then slowed as Bella's small canine head snapped up from its focus on a wayward moth and she ran to join him. She was an unusual Harlequin MinPin, black, gray and brown, rare on many levels. He smiled at her as he turned and continued to walk toward Youssef Bazzi's fate.

The small dog walked at his side just as she had for over a century. Whether or not he had a soul was still unknown to him. But, he had a companion, a purpose and a moral compass with flexibility he could live with.

"I'm done here after this I think," he said to Bella, eliciting a quick, excitable tail-wag. "I'm thinking a brief vacation in England and then head to America. See the New World now that it's older."

Bella barked her agreement and they walked the rest of the way, leisurely together, in companionable silence.

# The End

# FRANKENSTEIN'S
# COMPANION

# Author's Note

STARTED WRITING THIS short story in 2015 after I'd started writing my Blood Quill series (think Penny Dreadful meets Supernatural, modern day New Orleans, with a tiny bit of time travel). I knew that, one day, Adam would show up in New Orleans and he'd run into his old friend Victor Dracula. I was entertaining the idea of what Adam would be like if he had lived all through time.

I realized that, despite his large size and disfigurements, the modern world would be somewhat desensitized to that because the world had grown larger, saw more and didn't see such issues as witchcraft as something to immediately fear. He'd be like a wrestler with a gimmick, large and scarred. Some people would still look at him and not want to engage with him, but some would ignore him altogether because it was simplest to do so. Either way, he would go from being seen and feared to being unseen and alone. I needed him to have someone or something that enabled his compassion. Someone or something that let him know love was powerful. Someone to teach him the power of unconditional love.

About Bella. Bella is a Miniature Pinscher, or MinPin, which is actually not related to the Doberman Pinscher, but they do have similar markings. Bella is a Harlequin MinPin, which is more rare and very special. Please do Google it and look at what beautiful dogs they are. Bella is a real dog. Yes, there really is a Harlequin MinPin named Bella and she looks exactly as described in the Adam Frankenstein stories. She is not immortal, however. She is my dog. She is a rescue who came to me as a puppy with distemper. The likelihood, according to the vet, was that she would not survive and he offered to put her down so she'd not suffer. But, she was so full of spirit and had not had a seizure, so I was going to try and save her. I believed in my heart that she was one of those one-in-a-million and that she would survive.

It was a battle, but she never did have a seizure. She and I slept together, her on my chest, in the living room binge-watching the show Supernatural, for three months. And, she lived. She was the only animal from the shelter who survived that outbreak. I recall the night I thought we'd lose her and I held her all night, in my arms, whispering that she was a good girl and that, if love could save her, she would live forever. Love did save her. That and her incredible spirit. In my heart she is immortal.

# Dedication

*This book is dedicated to anyone who has ever cried against fur.
For those who love cats, or dogs or any pet that felt as though
they were your best friend. To those who understand just how
much a pet can become family.*

# Chapter 1

## London, England 1888

H E WAS SAVING HER life, and she shot him. The rain washed blood from his chest to his toes as it failed miserably to muffle the sound of her scream as he wrenched the pistol from her hand and pulled her to him, his arms a prison. The lightning struck the sky like a fist from a cruel god, illuminating the dark London alley. For a second the world was revealed in all its violent glory. The woman screamed again, not because of the dead man lying nearby, neck broken, but because the sight before her was a nightmare come to life. In that moment Adam Frankenstein, the creation of a madman and an evil witch, knew the woman he had just saved would have traded her savior for a villain without hesitation.

He covered her mouth, looking down into blue eyes that no longer saw hope of rescue, but mirrored every terror-filled face he'd ever seen. Or, rather, that had seen him. Adam searched for weeks to find her despite his loathing of the city and difficulties that came with needing to question, without being seen. A cloak could hide his disfigurements, but not his large size. Help was hard to come by even without the fear of a killer walking the streets, killing women in Whitechapel. He'd hired a man of unscrupulous morals, questionable methods but desperate financial predicament to help him in his quest. It led to finding the woman, but unfortunately the man kidnapped her from her lover's apartment to an undisclosed place while he negotiated a ransom for her release.

Adam glanced at the dead body again, pants down to his knees, ass glowing white in the darkness. Tram, or so the man called himself, apparently thought he would rape the girl, slit her throat and leave the blame to the Ripper as a way to prove he was not to be trifled with when Adam refused to pay up.

Lightning struck again and the woman fainted, saving him from another long, shrill scream. Limp in his arms, he picked her up, threw her over his shoulder and walked to the open mouth of the alley. The cold, the rain, the Ripper all kept the streets empty, though he felt eyes on him as he moved north where he had a covered carriage waiting. No one called out to stop him and no whistles gave him away to the police. Adam found the carriage just as he had left it, unmolested. He laid the woman inside, not bothering to put her on the seat, but leaving her on the floor. He considered tying and gagging her, but doubted she would be willing to leap from a moving carriage, so he shut the door, climbed up in the seat outside, took the reins and made haste out of the city.

The horses sped along the dark road unafraid of the lightning. Adam cursed his change of plans as one of the wheels hit a large rock jostling the carriage and causing him to twist in a way that tore at the wound in his chest. It was a three day ride to return the woman to her father, the man who had hired him. The old mage had requested The League of Supernatural Hunters, a group created by Adam's one and only friend, Mary Shelley, to help find the girl but she'd not been kidnapped, she'd run away and no supernatural being had been involved other than the father himself. The League refused him, but they owed him a debt from a previous mission in which the man had been useful in stopping a werewolf, so, knowing he was freelancing, they'd asked Adam if he wanted the job. Adam was never part of the League, but they had a common goal; kill creatures who posed a threat. The difference was, Adam included all creatures, not just those with supernatural abilities. He realized early in his life that humans were monsters too and that he had no prejudice regarding who or what needed killing.

The old mage had no money to speak of, but he would owe Adam a favor and sometimes favors were more valuable than money. The old man had recently lost his wife, so when his daughter ran away with one of the Queen's soldiers he'd become despondent and agitated, even frantic to find her. Adam cared little for the man's opinion of his daughter's lover, but the old man had shown no fear of Adam, offered him tea, food and respect, so Adam agreed to the terms.

"It is of the greatest importance to me that she is found immediately," the old man, Stefano Polleno, said, arms waving in the air, one hand pulling at his wild salt and pepper colored hair. "My Helena is fragile, sick. She's not recovered from the death of her dear mother. This solider has taken advantage of her, taken her from me when I need her most. He will use her and leave her to the dogs!"

In his agitation the man accidentally kicked the small dog that had been following him from one end of the large open room of the hut to the other. It yelped, stopping the man in his tracks and he picked the thing up. Adam had little knowledge of dogs other than the wild ones he'd come across. He knew humans often took them in as pets, but he'd not personally seen any this small. The creature was no larger than a loaf of bread and certainly no heavier than the crossbow slung across his back. It was normal in most ways, having four legs, a tail and fur, but it had unusual colors; primarily it was black and gray, but with tan markings on its face and feet. The small dark eyes peered at him, tail wagging as the man stroked its fur, apologizing for his carelessness.

"Oh, little Bella," Stefano cried, his Italian accent stronger with emotion. "Am I to hurt and lose you as well? No. No, I do not think you would leave me, my Bella. My loyal friend." He kissed the dog's head and sat her back down, looking at her as she sat at his feet seeming to hesitate for just a fraction of a second before looking back up at him. Stefano looked to Adam and managed a smile, less agitated after holding the dog. "Bella is my touchstone you see," he explained. "She calms me."

Adam, unused to conversation, answered, "The little creature is important to you."

"She has been my companion longer than any," he answered. "There is no love or loyalty like that of a dog. They care nothing for your station in life, your politics or …" he hesitated, looking at Bella, then Adam, "the way you look. They love you because it is their nature to love you. They would never leave you." The old man grew quiet, tears gathering in his eyes as he looked at the dog.

"Unlike people," Adam stated. If the old man was to be believed, the dog was unlike most people Adam knew, with the exception of Mary. People always judged you by the way you looked, by your station in life, by what they could get from you. And people, no matter how loyal, left you. Unlike Adam, people died. Adam had been created, the bastard son of science with magic as his whore mother. Immortality was the punishment for mixing the two to create new life from death. "But one day the creature will leave you. It will die."

Mary, the woman who'd helped him kill his maker and thwart the witch, Hannah, who'd helped bring him to life with her unholy magic, had died so recently Adam often forgot she was gone. That he was now friendless. The pain upon hearing such news had been unlike any he'd ever experienced. He'd been shot, stabbed, burned and stoned, all quite painful but none painful like the news of losing her. The other wounds healed, no scars to remind him of the pain he endured. But, the wound he carried inside him that rocked him to his very soul, it remained. Nothing healed it. He could ignore it for a time, but it was always there. Once he had thought being unloved and unwanted, a creature of horror too hideous to befriend, was a curse. Now, he thought perhaps it was just another tool in his arsenal to protect himself.

"No," Stefano spoke, taking Adam's attention. "No, not Bella. She is special, you see. When I was a young mage, learning magic from the old masters, I was given young Bella as my companion. But, she was attacked by the companion of another boy, his was a wolf, and my Bella was ripped apart." Stefano watched the small dog walk near the hearth where bowl of water stood and the little thing dipped its head to drink. "Her heart still beat when I carried her to the old masters. It was forbidden to kill another man's companion. The boy had found amusement in using his wolf to kill. That day they banished the boy and gave the wolf to one more deserving. They'd offered it to me, but I would only have Bella. And so one of the masters gifted me with a talisman, pushed into the bleeding body of the dog. He closed her wounds, leaving the talisman within her, making her immortal. And giving her special powers."

Adam considered the animal, which seemed to be considering him. Its eyes seemed to shine with intelligence and though the creature's tail wagged, Adam felt its scrutinizing stare watch him with keen interest.

"Special power?" Adam asked, intrigue sparking an idea.

"Yes. And you should know as we negotiate, Bella has the ability to detect lies," he said with pride.

"Useful." Adam watched the dog walk in circles before finally determining the spot was worthy to rest in. He smiled at the simple action so inherent to dogs.

"Yes, and she can shapeshift into a cat as well. That's useful when I need to leave her on her own. Cats are far more independent than dogs."

Renewed interest pulled Adam's attention back to the small animal who now lay in front of the fire, head on her paws, eyes closed. Her ears stood straight, her head slightly too small for her body, but not to the point that it was the first thing you noticed. The first thing Adam noticed upon closer examination of the creature was how soft her fur appeared. The gray and black mixed together, black spots scattered like large freckles, varied in size. He recalled a larger breed dog he'd seen with similar markings. The hunters came close to his home, so he tracked them to ensure they'd not stumble across his hut. They'd called the coloring blue merle, and though Bella was of a different breed, Adam felt confident the color was the same. Her legs were small, but long and fine, mostly the tan that also marked part of her face. She was a beautiful dog, but appeared unremarkable otherwise. She was immortal, just as he was, they were alike in circumstance, living on after others die, and neither of them human.

"I need my daughter to return to me soon. Before the next full moon to be certain. Do not give them enough time to plan their wedding and escape. My daughter is in mourning. She thinks she needs this young man to help her, but it can only end in disaster," Stefano said, wringing his hands and pacing once again.

"I want the dog," Adam blurted out. "I don't care why you want your daughter back. I would even kill the soldier if that's your desire. But, I want the dog as payment."

Stefano stopped abruptly. "Bella?" He was genuinely confused. "You want Bella? But, I cannot part with her. It simply isn't possible."

"Make it possible or find someone else to retrieve your daughter," Adam stated, calm and cold.

"I will give you one favor. A favor as agreed when you first arrived. I am a powerful mage. There is much I can give you." Stefano sounded panicked, lost and desperate. "I can make a potion for you that would cause you to appear handsome to those who look upon you. Or, give you a love potion so you may choose a wife. "

Stefano's offer was enticing. Adam desired a wife, but realized it would be difficult to find a woman willing to marry him, to be his companion. She would have to accept the way he looked and accept that her life would be forever in the shadows. He had long ago given up his need for acceptance by others, though he could admit that it would be good to walk openly among others without fear of rejection or violence. A wife, though temporary the situation would be as any wife he chose would someday die, would be welcome.

"I will think on this," he answered, causing the old man to release a deep breath he'd been holding.

"Good. Good. I have told you all I know of the soldier. You have the small portrait of my daughter. I am certain they are in London as that is where the young man's troop was headed. Make haste sir, collect her and bring her to me before the full moon rises and you will have your reward." Stefano handed Adam a cloth sack filled with bread and cheese and strips of dried beef. "This will help sustain you. You are welcome to use my horses if you would like."

Adam took the sack. "I have my own horses, thank you. I leave tonight. I will return as soon as I find her."

"Before the full moon. It is required, you understand?" Stefano asked.

"I understand."

It had taken two days to reach London in the black carriage pulled by Adam's two best horses. He arrived, secured a hotel room in a shady area of London, hired a man to help him and spent time locating the solider, his abode and then the girl.

Things went horribly wrong the first night Tram was to take the girl from the apartment she stayed in with the young man. The soldier was gone, the girl alone, no servant stopped Tram from entering the house and removing the girl. But, he was to deliver her to the carriage where Adam awaited. Several hours later Adam realized he'd been duped. He went to the apartment himself, found no one there, and then went back to his hotel room to await Tram and an explanation.

Later that night a knock on the door had Adam jumping from the bed to answer. The night clerk, dressed in a bowler's hat, brown tattered suit and wreaking of alcohol, handed him a letter.

"Mr. Tram asked that this be delivered to you this evening," the night clerk told him.

"When was it given to you?" Adam asked.

"An hour ago, sir," he answered. "He insisted that I wait an hour before bringing it to your room." He put the paper in Adam's hand, hands trembling, turned and trotted quickly down the hallway.

Adam opened the note, impressed that his hireling could write. The letters were printed like a child had written it, but he'd signed his name at the end of the brief missive.

*I have her. Bring gold. Tomorrow night meet beside the pub near your hotel.*

Adam threw the note to the floor, cursing. The man hadn't said how much gold to bring, but perhaps any amount would do. It didn't matter. Adam had no intention of bringing anything. The toad would get nothing from him but death.

He remained indoors, ordering his food to be delivered to the room. He considered visiting the brothel where the only whore in London willing to have sex with him resided. Adam saw her once a month, three days at a time. If he were to spend his gold anywhere, that would be the place. The whore was older, but still attractive and, more importantly, she was blind. She'd remarked on his size the first time he paid for her. She was more than willing to teach him what he wished to learn, give him what he longed to have and tell him what he needed to hear. But, the second time he visited her she was angry with him. She said he had hidden the fact that he was deformed and only after he left did her friends tell her what she'd just finished fucking. She demanded he pay twice the price. And he did.

Adam's patience wasn't forgiving and his temper was high. Becoming physical with anyone at the moment was likely not wise. So he remained in his room, waiting for night to fall. He waited another hour, dressed, threw on his dark cloak and packed his belongings. He would not be returning.

He went to the rooftop of the hotel after securing the horses a few streets away and paying an orphan boy to watch over them.

"You will have a coin now," Adam had told the young street urchin, "And three more when I return if the horses and carriage are still where I leave them. Five coins if they are ready to go and no harm has befallen them." He gave a single silver coin to the boy whose eyes shined bright at the round piece of hope put into his small hand.

"Right here," the boy pointed to where he stood next to the horses. "We'll be right here, no worries."

The boy could be no more than eleven, his face dirty,

his hair worse. His clothes were too small, tattered and smelled of filth. But, he'd been the only one not to run from him when he approached a group gathered beneath the awning of a building, out of the rain, but shivering. Adam kept his face hidden, but his hands were scarred at the wrists and his size struck fear into the hearts of most men. Still, the boy had remained, spoke to Adam and took the coin. Adam wondered what sort of life the boy had had that would make him so fearless. Or how hungry he must be.

Waiting on the rooftop now, rain pouring from the sky as though it would wash away the sins of London, Adam watched Tram pulling the girl into the alley, Tram's attention split between the entryway of the alley and the girl who fought him with surprising strength. She wrenched herself free and made to dart around Tram, but he brought his fist around and connected squarely to her stomach causing her to crumple to the ground. He kicked her in the ribs for good measure.

"Stay down there you bloody little bitch," Tram yelled. "If you get up, I'll kick your face in."

The cold burrowed inside Adam's coat, moving like a ghost through his clothes to kiss his skin, finding his flesh warm, but his response lacking. Unlike a man born of a woman, he was immune to extreme cold or heat, his body remaining the temperature he was created with, never changing inside or out. The rain carried the cold, exploding on contact, causing the humans below to shiver visibly as one hour lead to the next. When the bells of the clock tower rang out the witching hour, clanging in alarm, melodious only to those awaiting midnight, Tram pulled the girl to her feet.

"Bastard isn't willing to pay for you," Tram told her, "And if I release you, you'll have me in Newgate, hung and buried before the full moon rises."

The woman stood, swayed then pulled hard to break free of his grasp. The hours on the ground, her muscles growing cold, her dress gathering the weight of the water, slowed her movements and he grabbed her once more before she could take a single step away from him.

The crash of thunder heralded the lightning. Sound and light and cold came together to expose the violence below. Adam moved from rooftop to rooftop, moving in a single fluid leap to the mud and muck below.

Tram threw the girl against the side of the building, pushing up her muddy skirts then fumbling with the front of his trousers. "It's not gold, but I'll take my pay," he said, his lips against her ear, "And in the end they'll blame the ripper."

Adam moved from the shadows, the rain beating on dirt, brick and stone until it became a rhythm of violence echoing until nothing else could be heard. Moving slowly, becoming part of the darkness, unseen and deadly, the sound of his steps adding to the death song playing out in the alley. Focused on the man oblivious to all but his lust and anger, Adam reached out as the thunder roared, grabbing Tram around the neck, removing the man's ability to cry out as Adam's arm grew tighter crushing Tram's windpipe just before Adam pushed with his other hand, breaking Tram's neck.

Both bodies fell to the ground, but the woman pushed at Tram's to free herself. The sky lit up filling the alley with the first screams of the terrified woman. Adam stepped back, allowing her to gain her feet, though she pushed herself backward against the brick wall. There had been a time when Adam felt certain that saving a life would win him, not affection, but perhaps appreciation. So when she screamed he realized the hood of his cloak and fallen away, exposing his face and that nothing had changed for him. There would be no appreciation that he'd saved her from rape and certain death, there would be only loathing and fear. And like it was with the elements, he'd become immune, feeling nothing for her fear or pain.

Curiosity drew his attention to the object in her hand. Tram had brought a pistol, the girl had apparently found it when she crawled over his dead body. The weapon infused her with a measure of courage as she aimed it at him. Before he could reach out to take it, she fired into his chest, just below his heart. He rocked back, lost his footing in the mud and landed on his back. Pain blossomed, radiated out causing his lungs to pull a deep breath and his senses to focus all around him. The cold rain beat his face with every drop, the girl's mewling, her jagged breaths, even her beating heart filled his ears. He pushed his focus inward to the pain, searing, throbbing, but already beginning to burn with whatever magic kept such wounds from claiming his life. He assessed his ability to move, sat up and was on the girl before she could reach the light that cut into the mouth of the alley.

Adam had been grateful when the woman finally fainted. Now, hours into their journey he knew he would have to stop at his home, let his body heal, change his clothes and wait for the storm to pass. He would miss delivering her in time by one or two days, but she was alive and relatively unharmed. He'd return her and gain his reward.

The road he'd turned down was difficult to follow unless you knew it well. Brush and foliage reached out to embrace those attempting to pass by foot, horse or carriage. The wind whipped branches until they beat and scratched the carriage and Adam. He hunkered down, making himself as small as a man of his size could get. He pulled his cloak around him, but the branches tore through, slicing at his skin.

The narrow roadway opened gradually until it became a clearing that held a single hut, a small barn a shed and a small smoke house. He'd built it all himself. His personal sanctum. No one had ever crossed the threshold of his home except him. The calm that usually greeted him was replaced with trepidation, a cold stone in the pit of his stomach. He realized as the rain eased, but the wind picked up, he'd made an error bringing her here. He dismissed the idea of turning around and going elsewhere this late at night. The horses deserved rest and he needed to change his clothes. The pain in his chest had dulled, but the blood loss caused his body to crave rest.

Approaching the barn, a soft click followed by the banging of the carriage door as it was thrown open, caused Adam to pull back on the reins. The carriage lurched as the girl jumped out, landing several feet away. When Adam landed in the mud near her she took off in the opposite direction, dress weighing her down, but not stopping her progress.

"Damn!" Adam called out causing the horses to whinny. "No favor is worth this." He lurched forward, panting as though he'd already been running. "You've nowhere to run, woman," he yelled as he picked up speed. "I will not harm you." He wondered how long that statement would be true as he crossed from clearing to forest.

The forest was thick and dark. The trees were mostly bare, limbs reaching out to embrace those who would trespass. The wind whistled as it chased through those arms, rocking the limbs and even the trees themselves. The rain slowed as it bounced off the treetops and searched for its final landing. There'd been no stars and the moon which had peered through heavy gray clouds intermittently disappeared offering no assistance as he raced to capture the girl.

Adam had always been a hunter, senses honed to find, capture and kill. The snap of twigs and small limbs caused him to change direction. She was fast. Faster than he could have imagined under the circumstances. But, his legs were longer, his footing more sure and soon he heard her heavy breaths. Her hair was golden, her dress pale, and her movements out of rhythm with the swaying trees. When she was within arm's reach he leapt forward, pulling her to him, cushioning her fall as he lost his balance and landed on his back in the mud and thistle.

The weight of her body on his wounded chest forced a short groan from his lungs, but the deep, guttural growl was all her. She nearly brought him up off the ground as she levered herself, then tried to roll away taking him with her, his arms like steel around her midriff. Arms flailing, elbow repeatedly looking to connect with his body, he began to lose his grasp on her in an effort not to damage her. He pulled her back to him and rolled over, pinning her face down to the forest floor, Adam's full weight running along the length of her body.

"Be still," Adam commanded. "I'm not going to hurt you."

"You are hurting me you barbarian!" she replied, still thrashing beneath him. "I can't breathe with you pushing my face into the mud. Get off me!"

Adam eased his weight from her upper body, taking her arm and bringing it high behind her back, eliciting another growl. Her fist was nearly between her shoulder blades when he slowly got up, bringing her with him.

The wind blew leaves and nettles from their hair, but the mud would take more effort to be rid of. Adam pushed her forward, into his hut.

The spacious, simple domicile was sparsely decorated, two chairs between a single table, a long, narrow bed heaped with blankets took up one corner and next to it a side table stacked with books and a single, unlit candle. A tall shelf near a slow stove was filled with cooking utensils and plates. Clean, simple, functional.

Adam forced the woman into the chair furthest from the door. She was strong. Stronger than her petite frame would have one believe.

Pointing at her as he stepped away, Adam said, "Don't make me chase you again. If you try to escape, I will tie you to that chair."

She didn't move, but he thought it was partially due to the darkness within the hut. As he lit a candle he kept one eye on her.

"You've seen me, so further dramatics on that count are unnecessary. I am disfigured, not a demon. After speaking with your father, I believe you must have some education, so please apply it."

"My father?" she asked, her voice quiet, soft and childlike. "He wanted you to bring me back?"

"He is determined to have you back, yes." Adam struck the match, the horrible phosphorus odor wafting quickly throughout the hut before the light could fill the room. One oil lamp, industrial in size, gave off enough light to see much of the hut, but the edges outside the light danced in shadow. He sat the lamp on the table, taking the other seat nearest the only door. "I do not require reasons not to return you as they will not matter to me. He possesses something I desire and I will return you to secure it. It would be best for us both to remain here, out of the storm, tonight and return you in the morning. I will secure you to the bed and sleep in front of the door."

A few seconds went by before the expected soft sound of crying began. Adam watched her lie her head on her arms, shoulders shaking gently. He stood, but she didn't notice, or perhaps didn't care. He pulled a chest out from under his bed and opened it, removing clean clothes.

As he used a rag to clean off the muck and mud he began to dress, all the while keeping an eye on his reluctant guest. She finally sat up, but didn't stir to get up from the chair. She watched him, no screams now, but with detached interest as he stripped naked to complete his cleaning process before adding new clothes.

"My God, man! Must you remove your clothes in my sight?" Her voice wavered between what sounded like fright and anger.

"Close your eyes."

She grew silent as he completed dressing, looking out the small window as lightning lit the sky over and over again.

Adam pulled out a long night shirt from the trunk before putting it back under the bed. He thrust it at her, but she let it fall to the floor beside her.

"I don't care if you clean up or not," he told her. "But, you're welcome to that garment if you wish it. You will not be sleeping in my bed in muddy clothing, so consider that."

"I'll sleep on the floor." She continued looking out the window. "Or I'll not sleep at all."

"Suit yourself. I haven't the energy or inclination to beg you to take the bed. I will be tying you to it though, so I may rest without concern."

"You're a brute." She managed to look at him, this time anger replaced fear in her eyes.

"Yes."

"You think to profit from my misery, but tonight will be the last night you profit from anything." Her new-found bravado brought her shoulders back and she lifted her chin to make full eye contact. "My father," pain crossed her face before she continued, "can go to the Devil. And the two of you can plot from there."

Adam ignored the statement, stepping just outside the hut and returning with a length of rope. She visibly shivered at the sight of it, but made no move to elude him as he tied it to one leg of the bed and approached her, bending down to tie the other length to her ankle.

"Barbarian." She hit his shoulder as he bent over securing the knot. He ignored it, pulling hard to ensure it would be difficult for her to untie.

"Yes."

The storm raged on, thunder shaking the hut as though Satan knocked on the door. Lightning flashed often enough the lamp seemed unnecessary. The roof held and they remained dry. Cold slipped in through the cracks and Adam lit a small fire in the hearth.

"Do you require anything before I retire?" he asked.

She said nothing and he hoped she'd remain silent for the next few hours as he rested in the hope it would speed his healing process. He took a mug of water to bed and lay there reading for a few minutes before his hopes were dashed and the quiet crying began once more.

"You have no idea what you've gotten yourself into," she said, no emotion evident in her tone. "My father can't be trusted to keep his word. He has no money, regardless of what he's told you. You'll return me and he'll likely put some spell on you and you'll forget all you ever knew. He's a mage you know."

Pulling in a lungful of air Adam sat up, back against the wall of the hut. "Is there nothing I can do to keep you from speaking outside of gagging you?" he asked. "I realize you've lost your lover. You've been kidnapped and nearly raped and then kidnapped again. Regardless of your opinion of me, I am not the monster I may appear. Your father seems sincere in wishing you back with him without any hint of malice or intent to abuse you. He is your family. Not everyone has family. Go to him and try to put your differences behind you. Besides," he added, "I am not looking for money. I will be taking his dog as my payment."

A shrill laugh, short and dry, filled the air. "That dog is more valuable than even I. He will never part with her. Not even to have me returned to him. Not even to hide his wicked secret from the council of mages. The dog is immortal. It has an uncanny ability to ferret out lies from truth. It can shapeshift into a cat at will, or command, and as a cat she has a different set of abilities. No. You are a fool. He will use tricks, magic or weapons before he lets you have that dog."

"I am immune to most magic," Adam shared. "A condition of my creation. I am difficult to trick, as I've learned subterfuge and sleight of hand to survive. And I have no fear of weapons, as you have already seen that my wounds heal quickly. I am no fool."

She laughed again, but a hint of sadness hung within it. "He would give me to you, before giving you Bella. He uses the dog's blood for his experiments. It is what he would hide from the other mages. Among other things."

"I do not want you, I want the dog. An immortal companion, not bound by nature's rules. I care little for the dog's magic, its tricks. She will become my family and I will no longer be alone in the world. Whether he agrees to give the dog to me or not, I will take her." He felt no remorse and cared little for her judgment of him. He'd stolen before. First, out of necessity. Then, out of anger. Food, clothing, horses. Few would engage in commerce with a man such as him. Those who would look upon him in fear, disgust and hate would let him die of starvation if it were possible. They would let him freeze if it were possible. They had little compassion for one such as him and he had none for them. He would not kill to attain his desires, he'd promised Mary that much, but he had no remorse, no regret, for what he'd take to survive.

"I would help you take her," she offered.

"For your freedom?" he scoffed. The old mage would

not trick him, and neither would she. "I do not require your help to take the dog."

"I'd not do it for you," she said. "I'd do it for Bella."

Intrigued, he sat forward, the bed creaking beneath the movement. Lightning filled the room as thunder shook it. The storm was upon them, nature cursing them with an air of excitement and looming fate.

"Entertain me with your tale, then, woman. I will listen."

She picked up his night shirt as she stood and walked to the bed. She spread the shirt on the corner and sat on it, keeping her muddied clothes from his covers. Shoulders back, he knew her courage cost her much as he could feel the tremors of fear shake the bed at his feet.

"I love my father," she said earnestly, "but, I hate him, too." Her eyes boldly looked into his, no shrinking from the horrible scars she saw there. "He was better when mother was alive." She nearly whispered it, but then cleared her throat and lifted her chin before continuing. "He's a powerful mage, but his work in alchemy and the human body got him into trouble and he was thrown out of a powerful council of mages, given only the dog that had been gifted him. Bella. One of the greatest mages ever known had saved Bella's life when she was attacked. The dog was more than a gift though. She was a window for the mage council to watch over what my father was doing. Through magic the mage that saved her could see through her eyes. But, that was not told to father. Not until a few months ago when his experiment with Bella's blood cost the life of my mother."

The lightning struck, but had moved away from the hut and its light reached in with greedy fingers, desperately clawing through the window, winning no more than half the hut as it illuminated within. The sudden brightness cast additional light to one side of her face and, despite the mud and grime, she was lovely. Adam noted that she was fair where her father was dark and surmised that her mother must have been as she, yellow hair and alabaster skin. He wondered if her mother was an Englishwoman.

"So your father killed your mother during these experiments?" Adam asked.

"No," she whispered, her voice low and taking on a more sinister depth, nearly a growl as she let the word roll off her tongue. Lightning flashed fast and bright, bathing one side of her face and casting a most unusual hue of gold to her eyes. It lasted only a moment, and was gone with the current of energy it rode in on. The soft light from the table nearby flickered, the gold gone in an instant. "No, I killed her."

Adam leaned forward, the story more intriguing with a killer an arm's-length away. "So, was it a mercy killing then? Did he experiment on her and you released her from some horrific change, or pain?" Adam could understand that. He knew mercy killing intimately.

She turned her head away from the light and shadows hid her expression. Seconds ticked by and she pulled in air, held it a moment then slowly released it. Her shoulders sagged slightly as she faced him once more.

"I was ill you see," she began, "I was dying actually. Consumption. There was nothing that could be done. But, my father wouldn't give up. He studied science and magic and he was determined to save me. And my mother agreed that he should try. So night after night I was forced to drink some brew, drink some powdered concoction. I heard them argue over adding blood and flesh to the mix. I knew father was cutting Bella and putting some of her immortal blood in some of the drinks. I still have no idea what kind of flesh he used." She shivered visibly and wrapped her arms around herself for comfort or warmth. "At last my mother began to argue with him. But, he'd not stop. He would challenge God himself to keep me alive and I was far too weak to fight him. The final brew was thick as stew. I saw blood on Bella's throat." She stopped, covering her mouth with her hand as though to stop what would be said next. "He'd nearly drained her. The poor little thing could hardly walk. I know she is immortal, but if you'd seen her." She paused again and Adam waited. "Bella trusted him and he cut her over and over without thought. Father is like that. He loves you even as he hurts you. He hurt her and she would still come at his call."

"So the drink did something to you." Adam stated. "You're very much alive, so it must have worked."

Her smile was sad and she shook her head. "I lived, yes, but I'd hardly call it a success. I only remember the pain. Excruciating. It was as though I was on fire from the inside. My bones ached. At some point I fainted. The next thing I knew I was on the floor and my father was beating me with a cane. Bella was ripped apart, but alive. Mother was beneath me, shredded as though some demon beast had carved her with long claws."

She brought her feet up, her knees pulled to her chest. Her shoulders shook as she rested her forehead atop folded arms. In that moment Adam saw she was still young. A child blossoming into a woman, still innocent and naïve. Or had been. A few minutes went by and she began to unfurl. Wiping at her eyes, she continued her story.

"I was that demon beast who killed her," she announced. "The brew had turned me into something wild and dangerous. I was no longer human. I killed my mother and nearly killed my father."

Something softened within Adam's breast and wished he were the kind of man who could reach out and comfort her. But, he could not, so he kept silent, letting her take her time.

"For a few days father tried potions and all manner of magic in an effort to reverse what he'd done. I was locked away, tied up, because at night, the beast would come back. But, after a few days it seemed to lessen. I was brought back into the house for more experiments, but mother was gone and father was mad. The mage council sent someone to take me to London where they said there was a group of people who might help me. Father didn't want me to go. But by the time they came for me, I was ready to leave that house of death. I met with the mage, Sir Cartwright, late in the night and we fled."

"So, this Cartwright, he wasn't a lover?" Adam asked, recalling the story Stefano had given him.

She laughed without humor. "Sir Cartwright was older than my father. He was never anything but kind to me. He was angry with father, but he never showed anger to me. I believe he truly felt he could help me. Of course, he was killed by the man you sent to kidnap me." She glared at him. "Any hope of reversing this curse likely died with him. Who will help me now that they know they may pay with their life?"

Adam considered her story. If the dog could detect lies, could it also hide that someone is lying? Did the dog protect Stefano by not indicating his lies? He thought that was possible. And that was if he chose to believe the dog had that ability. Her story felt true. But, he had to acknowledge that his experience with people didn't give him any special insight to truth. To hate and judgment and fear, yes, but truth was tricky. Subjective.

"What would you ask of me?" Adam swung his legs over the side of the bed opposite her. "What is it you want?"

"I want you to take me to Italy, where the mage council is. Tell them Sir Cartwright was the victim of an unfortunate event and ask them to try and help me."

"You don't think your father will do this for you?" Adam stood and felt straw from the ground rub against the bottom of his feet.

"Father isn't allowed back there. And I know his experiments have made his return even less likely. His pride has already cost Sir Cartwright his life. He'll want to try and cure me himself, but I don't think he knows how. He had no confidence when he gave me potions he hoped would reverse my condition. And if he could cure me, I think Sir Cartwright would have left me there." She looked as though she would stretch out on the bed, then caught herself and sat up straight.

"You can lie on the bed as you are. I need to wash the bedding eventually. Get some rest. Let me think in peace." He sat at the table, glancing at the stove, contemplating the merit of coffee at this late hour.

She didn't hesitate and stretched out, taking one blanket to throw over her shivering body. "I can feel something happening inside me. The beast returning. Whatever it was father used to save me, he seemed convinced the magic was tied to the full moon. Tomorrow it will be full. We have little time to think, and even less time for peace."

Adam considered her unusual strength earlier that night. She was faster than most humans. He wondered what she would be like tomorrow when her beast was set free.

"No matter how this ends, the dog is mine." The old mage was willing to torture the small creature. He understood the man was trying to save his daughter and that the dog was immortal, but cutting its throat over and over was careless and cruel. When Bella became his, he would protect her. She would never be tortured again. A small but heavy weight lifted from within him. He would save her and care for her and she would be his loyal friend.

"Yes," she agreed. "The dog is yours, but you must agree to help me."

"The dog is mine regardless of what I agree or do not agree to. But, I will remain with you until there is an acceptable solution to what happens to you next."

Silence filled the room and spread out like the cold. The desperation in her voice pulled at Adam's senses and the need to protect her and the little dog filled his heart. Years of rejection and loneliness hadn't prepared him for the rush of energy coursing through his veins as he realized he was needed.

Adam listened to her even breaths as slumber found her. The storm diminished, echoes of thunder growing more and more quiet. He still listened to her as the sun rose a few hours later. The day brought sunshine and warmth. It was also the harbinger of night and the full moon and choices.

It was late in the afternoon when they reached the outskirts of Stefano's property. In the distance, just beyond the trees, a spiral of smoke reached for the clouds and Adam hoped the man had coffee waiting.

The woman allowed him to call her Helena, and she agreed to speak with her father before making demands or trying to run away. Adam would only agree to help her if she spoke with the old mage. If violence could be averted, that was his desire. Both Stefano and Helena had endured much tragedy. If they could be spared further pain, Adam would leave them in peace. He would not leave without Bella, however. So whether peace could be attained, and maintained, was difficult to predict.

Wind blew gentle, then stronger as they approached. Leaves had long since met their doom in the mud. Naked branches seemed to reach for them as the lane narrowed and Stefano's home came into view.

"He will want his way in all things," Helena warned. She'd cleaned up and did what she could to tame her wild, yellow hair. Her clear, white brow furrowed as Stefano peered out at them through the window. "He may have some trap set for both of us."

"Perhaps." Adam agreed. "So it is best that we make your wishes known right away and gauge his reaction."

Adam watched Stefano disappear from the window. Bella's nose peered out at them as she struggled on her two back legs to stand tall enough to watch them.

He helped her down from the carriage and tied the horses nearby as she waited for him. The front door opened, but Stefano didn't come out. Instead he moved away, leaving the door open for them. Helena glanced back at him, worry in her eyes, but she preceded him inside.

The sun shone down on him, blinding him at the moment he stepped inside the dark interior of Stefano's home, but his senses, heightened first by the nature of his creation, but even more so by the potential of danger from Stefano, he heard the quickened intake of breath before it was stifled. Adam turned toward the sound, which now echoed with the scraping of wood and rustling of clothes, just as white-hot pain seared into breast, through flesh and bone, burning once more at his back. Instinctively, Adam turned in the direction of the sound as he grabbed the long, thick arrow, caring little for how it ripped as he pulled it out.

Another arrow caught him in the shoulder, but he'd stepped further inside and his eyes registered movement to his right. He swung with speed and strength knocking another arrow from the air. Eyes adjusting, three shadowed figures caught his attention. One, held the slight figure of Helena. Captured, she struggled to free herself and, as Adam grabbed the man holding a crossbow, Helena broke free.

Stefano stumbled back, struggling to capture her

once more, but Adam couldn't help. A large, strong man dropped the crossbow as Adam took hold of it and reached in for a dagger so sharp Adam didn't feel the first slice across his palm. The dagger arched high in the air, but Adam blocked his attack by pushing up with his forearm, moving the man's arm to the side where it connected with a surprised Stefano. The dagger fell when the man's knuckles connected with Stefano's cheek. Adam kept the momentum and pushed into the man's side, driving him back hard enough the man hit the wall behind them, the sound of several ribs cracked loud enough Adam could hear it.

"Stop!" Helena screamed, causing Adam to turn.

Stefano had the dagger in his hand, the tip nearing Adam's throat. Before Adam could turn his attention to Stefano, Helena caught her father's arm and pulled him back, causing him to fall, with her beneath him.

The man at the wall pushed his body forward into Adam's, but the adrenaline coursing through Adam's veins added speed to his strength and Adam caught the man, threw him up in the air and down next to Stefano.

Adam picked up the fallen crossbow, loaded it and trained it on the men in the floor. "Let her up."

Helena pushed Stefano to one side and crawled from beneath him. Taking her place at Adam's side she picked up the dagger and stood tall and ready to fight.

"I don't understand," said the man in the floor, the one who'd helped Stefano ambush them. "Why would she help you if you killed her mother?" Slightly out of breath, the man sat up, holding his side. Casting a glance at Stefano, the man grimaced, jaw flexing as clenched teeth bit down through the pain.

It took Adam a moment to realize the man was speaking to him. Whether it was some tactic to distract him or a sincere question he was unsure, but the man hadn't pulled out another weapon, so Adam answered. "I did not kill her mother."

"He is a murderer! A kidnapper!" Stefano cried out as he stood.

"He is not," Helena spat at him, her anger etched across a furrowed brow. "He did not kill my mother. He did not kidnap me. He is here to help." She drew back as though willing to use the dagger if either man approached.

Adam found it prudent not to argue with her, though in fact, he had killed Tram and had taken her from London against her will to return her to her father. Facts notwithstanding, he was in a position of power with the weapons and a soon-to-turn-beast woman of immense strength beside him. Facts at this point were nearly irrelevant.

The large man stood and though he was not as tall as Adam, he was tall. Long, dark hair, pulled back and secured, he appeared young, not yet twenty and five, though his build was bulked with muscle giving him the air of someone older. Stefano stood behind him, not daring to take up the fight while weaponless.

"You are Helena?" The man asked. When Helena nodded the man continued. "I am St. John of the mage council. Your father's familiar alerted us to danger and when Cartwright did not return, I was sent to find out what happened. Cartwright was able to use the dog to see, but I haven't that ability. Where is Cartwright?"

"Dead," Helena told him. "Killed by a man in London who tried to rape me."

"Bella," the man called and the small dog entered the house from outside. Bella hurried to Helena, licking her face when Helena knelt down to greet her. "So Cartwright was not killed by the man standing next to you?"

"No, he was not." Helena stood, glancing at Bella before looking defiantly at the man.

Adam watched the dog for signs of communication

knowing the creature's power to detect lies. But, of course Helena had not lied. It was Tram who'd killed Cartwright. Truth had its loopholes.

Watching the dog, St. John nodded and his shoulders visibly relaxed, though he continued to hold his side as though he were keeping the broken ribs from doing more damage as he moved, taking a seat at the nearby table.

"He is a murderous creature," Stefano argued, approaching St. John until the man put out a hand to stop him.

"He is something not of man, I can see that for myself," St. John said. "What he is, I do not know. Perhaps he can explain?" St. John looked at him, curiosity warring with pain.

"What he is doesn't matter." Helena stepped forward. "If you know Cartwright then you knew his mission and that my father was doing experiments, just as the council forbade him to do. Cartwright arrived over a fortnight ago and learned that I had been dying of consumption and my father concocted a potion that turned me into a beast. It was I who killed my mother. And I will kill again this night if I am not shackled and locked away. When my father refused to allow Cartwright to take me to London where he thought I could find help, we were forced to leave without father's permission. So, father hired this man to retrieve me, promising him anything, lying to him, and in the end, trying to kill him and make it appear he'd murdered my mother."

"If I murdered the mother, and this Cartwright fellow, and kidnapped Helena, why would I return?" Adam asked, intrigued at the web of lies Stefano had hoped to weave.

"To collect the ransom," St. John said. "An exchange. The daughter for the dog. The dog eluded you, so you took the daughter instead. In your rage you killed the mother. Cartwright went after you to save Helena and you murdered him."

"A carefully crafted story." Adam said, "But the only truth of it is that I do plan on taking Bella."

Helena nodded. "I told him that I would help him claim Bella if he helped me. Father can't cure me. And I would rather die than kill innocent people. Adam was to take me to the council and keep me from killing."

St. John eased back slowly in the chair. Stefano paced back and forth in front of the table, pulling at his hair until the short, gray strands stood on end. Adam felt the air grow thick with tension as St. John appeared deep in thought. Adam wished only to hand the woman over to the mage so she could find help and then leave with the dog as his reward. St. John's contemplation inferred the man thought his judgment would be final law. Adam hoped he'd not have to kill the man, but his hands tightened on the crossbow when St. John stood, gaining the attention of all in the room.

"Stefano, I cannot imagine what it must be like to watch your child dying. And the grief of losing your wife has taken a toll on your ability to make sound judgment. But, the terms of the mage council were clear and you were not to experiment as you did. In the end, you exchanged your wife's life for your daughters, and abused Bella during your madness." St. John started to sigh, but grimaced and breathed shallow once more, adding pressure to his side.

The warmth of the sun filled the small home until Adam longed for a reprieve from the heat. The small home held a sour odor, that of sickness and despair. Bella remained at Helena's feet, watching St. John just as everyone else did.

St. John looked at Adam. "What are you? Man, beast? You appear as a man, but surely you are more?"

Adam felt the scowl crease his forehead. It would be nothing to simply take the dog and fight his way out. His only hesitancy was whether or not the dog would accept him should he steal it. He had no experience with pets and if she held a grudge, she might just run away at the first opportunity.

"I am a man, made of flesh," Adam answered, "But not born of a woman."

"I see that you have not harmed Helena, and indeed I see you would protect her."

"Your point?" Adam grew weary of St. John's scrutiny.

"You have kept your end of a bargain." St. John pinned Stefano with a glare, stopping whatever words were about to escape the old mage. "As I represent the council I am at liberty to complete the bargain where the dog is concerned. I release the dog to you to own without interference as long as you treat her well."

"No!" Stefano yelled, causing Helena to step back, nearer to Adam. "Am I to lose all? Everything? Is that my due?"

A dull ache spread within Adam's chest as he watched the man whither until he sat on the floor. Helena rushed to him, kneeling and taking him to her.

"He will not be punished?" Adam asked, finding that it mattered and feeling surprised at his feelings. The old man lied to him. Manipulated him. Would have killed him. But, something deep inside of Adam wished he could stop the man's pain. Adam knew too well the dangers of despair.

St. John looked at father and daughter, his own eyes moist and shining. "They will both return with me. Stefano is a gifted alchemist. I will speak to the council and ask that he be allowed to remain with us until we are able to free Helena of her curse. It is the best I have to offer."

Adam nodded. Helena, absorbed in her grief, rocked her father gently like a child in her arms. Stefano held to her, tight and desperate. He cried softly, but said no more of his fate.

"You are free to leave," St. John said. "You have a companion who will care for you. Be loyal. Be good."

"I can promise only to try," Adam said.

St. John smiled as he said, "I was speaking to Bella."

Adam had no reply. He turned to retrieve the dog, but she was beside him, deep, brown, intelligent eyes looking up as she wagged her tail.

Adam walked out into the sunshine and opened the door of the carriage for the small dog. She looked at him for a moment, the jumped up into the driver's seat to wait for him. The carriage swayed as he took his seat.

Slowly, he reached out, using one finger to caress down her neck and back. "Soft," he said to her. "I knew it."

She leaned into him and he pet her head as he'd seen the old mage do. Warmth tingled from his fingertips and spread to his chest. "You're beautiful." A knot seemed lodged in his throat and he cleared it, but it remained. She put a paw on his thigh, stretching to reach the top, licked his hand and looked up at him. He knew little of pets, but he would have sworn she smiled at him. The warmth in his chest grew and he pet her fur over and over.

The warm wind picked up and the promise of a cold night wove within it. Adam took the reins and headed toward home.

"I will take care of you as long as we both live," Adam promised. "Do you believe that?"

Bella barked, tail wagging and rested her head so she could look up at him.

Petting her once more before putting his focus on the road ahead he whispered, "I am not alone."

# The Therapist
## and the Dead

# Author's Note

I'VE BEEN FORTUNATE ENOUGH to visit Brooklyn, NY many, many times. I love the city and its people immensely. But, back in the 1980's things were vastly different and the city was a harsher place than it is now. But, its people remain much the same. People of Brooklyn are loyal to a fault and have very little tolerance to bullshit, which they will call you on. Gentrification pisses them off and they are proud of their history. Brooklyn is an amazing city and I highly recommend visiting there.

# Dedication

*This is for Charina Russo of Brooklyn, NY. She is fiercely loyal to family and friends. She's protective of all the things she loves.*

*Including her city.*

# Brooklyn, NY

## November 1982

THE SNOW DANCED ALONG the wind, becoming nearly iridescent as it spiraled from shadow to a street light where it swirled in the spotlight and out again. Adam Frankenstein paused on his walk from Bay Parkway near Ft. Hamilton in the park and looked at the large cannon, a monument to the still-operational military fort. Looking at the starless sky and gently falling snow he marveled at the uniqueness of Brooklyn with its loyalty to the past. The Verrazano Bridge could be seen from where he stood, even if just a portion and he wished one day to walk the length of the bridge, that marvel of man, stretching longer than the Golden Gate by 60 feet. Perhaps one day, he thought. Currently it only allowed vehicles to cross it except for special occasions.

The weather in Brooklyn was as dependable as its people. Winter announced itself even though it wasn't officially here yet. At 8 o'clock in the evening night was truly upon the city, dark and cold and dangerous. Though, as Adam grew nearer to Bay Ridge, tonight's destination, the criminal activity thinned. Perhaps there was less criminal activity because of the cold, though Adam guessed it was between 35 and 40 degrees out, certainly not cold enough to close down this city. It could be because the more upscale area of the city, in which he now walked, was better patrolled by police. Likely, it was that today was the day after Thanksgiving and many were either on holiday or still enjoying the peaceful respite and gentle remembrances that this uniquely American holiday represented. Even criminals had family who loved them, he mused. They had homes to go to and people who wanted them.

Adam continued walking, picking up the pace so his companion wouldn't be out in the cold much longer. She had grumbled over his choice of her attire, finally accepting the sweater but completely refusing the footwear regardless of his insistence. Glancing over his shoulder he saw her hanging back a few feet, still angry about being forced to do something she didn't want to do, punishing him by refusing to walk beside him.

"Bella," he grumbled. "Stop pouting and get up here."

The ten pound Harlequin Miniature Pinscher stopped and sat down in defiance. The small dog had been his only companion for over a century and they understood each other.

Adam stopped and turned to face her. "Get over it. It's cold out and you need to wear something warm. It can't be helped that there's a pink poodle on your sweater. We work with what we've got."

She barked, bringing a puff of white into the air from her warm breath which did nothing to encourage Adam to remove the offensive sweater.

"Okay, once we get to Dr. Stein's office I'll take it off," he relented. They understood each other alright. Bella understood she was in charge and Adam understood she was right. He just couldn't let her know he understood. "But when we leave, it goes back on."

She hesitated, as though considering the offer, then stood and slowly caught up with him as he turned and continued on his way.

As he watched the pavement beside him turn to cobblestone he knew he'd made it to Bay Ridge. A line of homes, similar in structure; limestone, beveled fronts, tall stairs to the doors all encased in a line of black metal fencing and gates, lined the street as far as he could see. Bay Ridge was called Doctor's Row by some, but most people recalled the area from a famous movie released not long ago called Saturday Night Fever.

Where Bay Parkway had very little holiday decoration, Bay Ridge had started celebration of Christmas early. Multi-colored holiday lights wrapped around step rails or atop fence railing, some blinking cheerily in the dark cold, some simply lighting the way for pedestrians. Some of the small gates had large red ribbons tied to them; several doors had wreaths of holly or silver bells.

Adam couldn't help noticing the flurry of activity within the homes, curtains left partially open, inviting passersby to peek into their joyful lives. Children laughing as they helped decorate a tree, a couple dancing to Christmas music. In one of the homes a window was partial lifted allowing the aroma of apple pie and caramel to drift out and ride the wind over to him and Bella. Looking down at her he smiled as she lifted her head to sniff the air.

"Smells good," he said, and continued walking.

Adam watched the numbers on the houses as they descended. Stopping, he turned to look at the home of Dr. David Stein. Stein's home was devoid of decoration, but the light over the doorframe was bright and the stairs well lit. The doctor's curtains were closed with heavy drapes giving no hint as to whether lights were on or off within. Looking further skyward, the second story windows were equally covered.

"Dr. Stein is very serious about his privacy I think," he said as he and Bella walked through the small gate and headed up the steep concrete stairs.

The door was black with brass fixtures. The numbers over the door were brass, the doorknob, the mail slot and the decorative doorbell. Adam pressed the button and heard footfalls immediately. The door swung open and a tall thin man with a long beard and mustache, dark eyes and high forehead peered out at them, a frown etched across his face that deepened when he looked down at Bella.

Adam picked her up, producing a handkerchief from his pocket and began cleaning her paws as he waited for an invitation to enter.

"You're late," Stein said, making no move to allow Adam in. Instead he closed the door just a little, partially hiding himself and looking Adam up and down suspiciously.

"As you can imagine, I have a difficult time getting a taxi to stop for me. My size is intimidating and my face, well…" Adam leaned further into the light, allowing the doctor to see his scarred face.

Stein shut the door another inch, leaving only his head sticking out. "Yes, well, be that as it may, you're half an hour late, so we'll need to reschedule." He looked at Bella once more. "And I don't allow dogs into my home. Dogs are dirty and ill behaved."

"Not *my* dog," Adam assured him, setting Bella at his feet and patting her head. "Tonight is the only night I have."

The man moved back as though Adam had thrown something disgusting at him, and then realized the movement caused the door to open wider and moved back to his former position. Adam watched the man's hand move over his chest, rubbing as though to soothe. As though stressed to pain.

"Mr. Frank, regardless of the money, no therapist can be expected to truly help you if you are planning on having only one session," he assured Adam. "It's ludicrous to think otherwise."

Adam began to feel warmer from the inside out and he clenched his jaw over and over while considering his next move.

"You misunderstand me, Dr. Stein." Adam drew in a lungful of air, letting it out in a slow line of white fog. "What I mean is that this is the only time I'm willing to meet with you to determine our relationship. If you are unavailable this evening I'll not be returning."

The man appeared struck, his brows knitting together, the corners of his mouth downturned. "Do you know who I am?"

"I do," Adam answered. "Which is why you are my first choice. You are, however, not the only choice. So, though I'd certainly prefer you, if you don't feel you can accommodate me, I understand."

The door opened slightly as the man considered this. Adam had the feeling Stein had made up his mind, but was allowing them to stand out in the cold as evidence of his ire. From within the house Adam could smell chicken soup and fresh baked bread, and underneath that was the odor of bleach, or some similar chemical.

"The price is double for the inconvenience and for the dog," he stated. His brows, now highly arched looked at Adam in challenge.

"You doubled your normal price to meet at your home and doubled it again to meet at night. Are we doubling it once more because I brought my dog?"

"You are the one, a stranger, asking to do your session in my private home, at much inconvenience to me. Then you show up late when you should have known you'd have difficulties with transportation. You've already informed me that you've been disfigured for years, so I know you realize your own challenges. You don't bother asking me how I feel about having an animal in my home. For all you know I have an allergy or a fear of dogs. I am happy to accommodate you, but you must be equally happy to accommodate the price for getting what you want, the way you want, at the time you want."

Adam let the seconds tick by before answering. "I hope you're as good as I've been told. You have a deal Dr. Stein."

"I'll need the check tonight, or course." He slowly opened the door and stepped back allowing Adam and Bella to enter.

"Of course," Adam answered.

Once inside, Dr. Stein took Adam's leather jacket and hung it on a coat rack in the hall. Adam removed Bella's sweater and stuffed it into one of the jacket's pockets. Bella shook her body and wagged her tail in triumph.

"Follow me into my study. Everything is set up there." Dr. Stein brought them down the hall where Adam noticed several commendations, certificates, works of art, but no family photos. There were, however, several stuffed birds mounted and encased in displays along the way, leaving Adam to wonder if the chemical odor he smelled was diluted formaldehyde, or some other chemical associated with the art of taxidermy.

The study was located on the first floor. Once inside, Dr. Stein motioned to an overstuffed chair that appeared to have been moved into the corner so that it sat beside Dr. Stein's large desk. The mahogany desk had a colorful Paradise Parrot mounted on a small perch on the side of the desk furthest from Adam. A large empty space near a tall floor lamp, next to a stack of books, is where Adam thought the chair normally lived. He took the seat, Bella immediately making herself comfortable on the rug near his feet.

Dr. Stein looked at Bella for a moment, but instead of commenting on her he said, "Would you care for some tea perhaps?"

"No, thank you," Adam answered. He and Bella had

taken their meal at the hotel and, as a rule, didn't accept drinks from strangers unless the drinks came sealed.

As Dr. Stein took his seat at the large desk he pulled a file from the top and opened it. Adam saw his name, an alias, written on the manila file.

"I see you received the paperwork I faxed earlier this week," Adam said.

Dr. Stein peered over the file. "Yes, it's a great deal of information. I've had a chance to read it all. I've made some notes here that I'll be referring to in a moment." Dr. Stein had a cup on the desk already and he picked it up, sipped, and set it down again. "What I don't see here, or at least what's not exactly clear to me, is what specifically you are here for, Mr. Frank?"

Adam smiled, relaxing back into the chair. The aroma of Orange Pekoe tea wafted through the air and Adam breathed it in, savoring it. He was more of an Earl Gray man when he drank tea, but loved the smell of fruit, any fruit. He always had.

Somewhere in the house, above them, but not directly, music played. Adam recognized the song; Steve Miller Band's Abracadabra, which surprised him since he had Dr. Stein pegged as a classics man.

"Is there someone else here?" Adam asked. "I hear music."

Stein's eyes cut straight to the roof for just a moment. "No. I must have left the radio on."

A low growl from the floor brought Adam's attention to Bella. Her gaze was focused on him, communicating with raised hackles and eyes that shined in the minimal light. Adam held her gaze a few seconds. "Bella," he said quietly, not a reprimand, but more a release command. She remained in place, but grew quiet once more.

"I'm sorry, Dr. Stein, what was the question again?" Adam relaxed back once more.

"Is there going to be trouble with your animal?" Stein

asked, a worried look crossing his face as he leaned to the side in an attempt to see her.

"Bella is fine, doctor," he assured the man. "I believe I recall the question. You asked what specifically brought me here, correct?"

Stein sat upright once more, sipped his tea and answered, "Yes, from your rather significant list of issues, I'm unclear as to what exactly you'd like to work on. I see issues with your parents."

Adam interrupted, "I have no parents."

"I understand that they are deceased, but here you refer to them as your makers. A very sterile way to refer to your parents." Adam started to respond, but Stein moved on. "Are you wishing to discuss your relationship with them?"

"Not particularly, no." Adam answered. Looking around the room as Stein referred to his notes Adam spotted a group of vintage books. "Do you read the great philosophers, Dr. Stein?" Adam motioned to the books. "Plato, Aristotle, Socrates, Confucius," he read them off. "But, you don't have Nietzsche. He was quite the interesting fellow."

Dr. Stein glanced at the books for a moment, and then set Adam's file down on the desk. "I read that you are an agnostic. As a man who finds Nietzsche an interesting fellow, do you agree with him that God is Dead? Are you in a crisis of faith?"

Adam crossed his legs, then uncrossed them and shifted forward in his chair. "I was born in a crisis of faith, doctor. But, no, to answer your questions, I do not believe God is dead. I believe Nietzsche had a problem with the church and that extended out to God. He was brilliant and confused and died a shadow of his former self."

"So are you an admirer of only Nietzsche, or of all philosophers?" Stein asked.

"Understand, I admired Nietzsche, but I disagreed

with him in equal measure to that in which I agreed. I found him fascinating, and enjoyed him. But, I do admire other philosophers as well. A deep and critical look at who we are as individuals and together, reflections on what drives us or makes us feel or react, it's all interesting to me. Human nature examining itself, devoted to wisdom, seeking it, trying to understand it."

The music upstairs changed and Joan Jett sang about her love for rock n' roll. A loud thump as though a book or other object fell on a carpeted floor jolted the doctor from his chair.

"Excuse me," he said, and then rapid footstep ascended to the second floor leaving Adam and Bella alone for several minutes.

"Bella," Adam said her name and she was at once alert. "I need you to go upstairs and see what the doctor has going on up there."

She stood, but footsteps descended and the doctor rounded the corner, his expression hard to read. Bella lay down quietly as the doctor took his seat.

"We'll not be disturbed by music now," he promised.

"And the loud noise?" Adam questioned.

"A window was open and the breeze knocked something over."

Bella's low growl and accompanying raised hackles gained her Adam's attention, but he shook his head at her and she quieted again.

"Mr. Frank, as I don't have much more time, let's get down to it, shall we? What has brought you to me?"

"A ghost," Adam told him, waiting for Dr. Stein to flip through his file, likely buying time to reply.

He sat the file down once more and sipped his tea. "Tell me about this ghost."

Adam sat forward, elbows on knees, pinning Stein with a serious gaze. "It's not often I'm visited by spirits.

I'm often an enigma to them and, like people, they tend to stay clear of me. But, a few weeks ago I began dreaming of a young boy. Eight or nine perhaps, with blond hair and black eyes. Though the boys eyes could have been any color before he was dead. Most ghosts I've encountered have nothing but blackness where their eyes once were." Stein said nothing, so Adam continued. "I saw him in a forest at first, then he moved and I knew he was in New York when I saw the Brooklyn Bridge behind him. Persistent, the boy returned again and again until I could no longer sleep. Each visit he grew clearer in my mind's eye. Each time his clothes were dirtier, or perhaps singed. Then, last week, he spoke to me."

Dr. Stein held up his hand and Adam stopped. "Do you feel this boy is you?"

"No." Adam answered.

"Do you know who the boy is?"

"No."

"What do you believe the boy represents?"

Adam stood and walked the length of the doctor's bookshelves, stopped where the collection of philosophy books were displayed. "Did you know that Plutarch believed in the supernatural?" He didn't wait for an answer, but made his way back, stopping in front of the doctor's desk. "Even brilliant men know there's something beyond the grave."

"Does the boy represent the supernatural to you?" Stein asked.

"I believe the boy *represents* nothing. He is delivering a message." Adam took his seat as the doctor reached for his tea. "He is a murdered boy and wishes me to search for his brother."

Dr. Stein coughed, setting his tea back on the desk. He cleared his throat, wiping his mouth with the back of his hand. "And do you truly believe you are seeing ghosts, Mr. Frank?"

"I believe that each night, when I look for solace in

slumber, a fair-haired boy in a school uniform visits me to make a request. It's the same request each time."

Stein looked at a clock on the far wall. His eyes cut to the ceiling and he turned his head slightly as though listening. Swallowing hard he sat back in his chair, picking up a pen that he began to click open and shut.

"You're having a difficult time sleeping, which I can give you a prescription for, of course. Reading your file, it's not hard to understand where the dream originates from. You're an orphan yourself, left to a cruel world which will not accept you due to your unusual disfigurement and size. You long to be small, an innocent child, enlisting help from someone stronger than you." Stein rushed the words together, sipped his tea, hands shaking until he threw the pen on the desk, and swallowed hard.

Above him Adam could hear the pitter-patter of Bella's feet as she went from one room to the other, but the doctor didn't hear, he focused on the clock, on his tea, on anything but furthering the conversation, so Adam responded. "Each night the boy asks me to find Frederick. Find his brother and take him home."

Stein gasped, his cup falling to the floor. "Who are you?" he demanded, standing so quickly that his chair tipped over behind him.

Two sharp barks sounded and Dr. Stein started around his desk, eyes cutting between Adam and the sounds above. Adam moved, blocking him in.

"Tell me about Frederick," Adam kept his voice calm as he gently guided the doctor back, picking up his chair. "I know he's upstairs, locked in a room."

Red moved up the doctor's neck and into his face, but Adam wasn't sure if the man was enraged or about to have a heart attack. The wetness in the man's eyes caught the light and shined, giving him the appearance of one fevered with fear.

A door opened above and Bella's excited barks became muffled as the door closed again.

"He won't harm your dog," Stein said, reaching into a top drawer and bringing out a small flask. "Freddy likes dogs. He's likely thrilled at the intrusion." Removing the top he drank deeply from the flask.

"Is the boy alright? " Adam asked. He realized the boy had not been locked away or he'd not have been able to admit Bella into his room.

"You tell me, Mr. Frank," Stein answered. "You're the one communing with ghosts. What did Albert say?"

"Albert? Is that the name of the other boy? He never told me his name," Adam felt the fine hairs on the back of his neck stand at attention as the temperature of the room dropped significantly. "Tell me what you did to them."

Stein looked around the room as though waiting for an apparition to appear, but it was no longer fear in his eyes, it was altogether something else, but Adam couldn't name it, so he asked again. "What did you do to Albert and Frederick?"

"Do?" he asked Adam, confusion causing his eyes to grow large and round. "I loved them."

Bella barked, a child laughed and Adam wondered what kind of love left one boy dead and another imprisoned in an unlocked room. Adam moved the large chair directly in front of Dr. Stein and took a seat. "I was sent here by a dead boy to save his brother," Adam began, "But, how he died was not revealed. Perhaps you can enlighten me on this?"

Dr. Stein drank again from the flask before setting it down on the desk with shaky hands. "God *is* dead, Mr. Frank, just as Nietzsche said." Stein looked at Adam, but the man's eyes seemed to look *through* him, seeing something not in the room. His words puffed out on white clouds, the cold more prominent than it had been out in the new-falling snow. "Albert and Frederick were twins. They were very special. You see, Albert was unusually bright, quiet and thoughtful. Frederick was born with Down Syndrome, simple but so outgoing, so loving, especially close to his brother. Other than sharing a womb, they seemed completely different from one another, but they were inseparable.

"They were born in the late 1960's and as the boys grew older their mother opted to home school them, so they could remain together. But, it was far more difficult than she imagined, I think. So, in the early 1970's as advocacy groups began to insist on the rights of the mentally disabled and laws began to change, she opted to allow them to attend school together."

Something about Dr. Stein's statement caused Adam to pause, but he hadn't the time to examine it yet and wanted the doctor to continue, which he did.

"Back then, the schools segregated people like Frederick from the rest of the student population. Laws continued to evolve, but New York was slow to adapt and their mother, Ruth, began to pressure the system. She was a fighter, Ruth." Stein paused a moment, smiling at the recollection. "Albert had exceeded all expectations in school and was a crown jewel there, winning academic scholarships by the time he was eight. Unheard of! They wanted to place him in a special school for gifted boys, but Albert wouldn't leave his brother behind. Oh, they pleaded with Ruth to encourage the boy to take advantage of such an opportunity, but she'd not be swayed. And she grew more angry about how little was done for Frederick. She fought so many battles with that school and with Frederick's teacher." Stein's far away gaze narrowed, scowling as he mentioned the treatment of Frederick, jaw clenching as he spoke of Frederick's teacher.

Laughter filtered down to them, Bella barking and

running back and forth as though the boy were perhaps throwing a ball for her to fetch.

From his peripheral vision, Adam saw movement from the hall, a shadow that disappeared up the stairs before he could turn to identify it. The cold receded and for a moment Adam wished for a flask of his own as quiet, even footsteps climbed the stairs. A momentary worry for Bella gave way to curiosity as Stein continued, clearly oblivious to the addition of a visitor.

"Ruth was to attend a parent-teacher meeting one evening and begged me to come with her. She wanted me to make it clear that the boys needed to remain together. She was tired of being harassed about moving Albert to another school and angry at Frederick's teacher for refusing to allow Albert to visit his brother during recess, which they'd done the year before. She thought I could somehow sway them with my credentials." Stein glanced out at the hallway where so many certificates and commendations hung.

Adam heard the opening and closing of the door upstairs. Bella barked, but there was no distress in her voice. Giggling laughter filtered down and Adam heard whispers.

"You look awful Albert." One boy, presumably Frederick, laughed.

"You smell awful, Freddy." Albert challenged good-naturedly.

Stein shook his head as though clearing his memory. "Did you say something?" he asked.

It was quiet above, except for Bella's running, chasing and barking as though she was having the time of her life. Bella had always been fond of children, seemed to actually prefer them, with the exception of Adam.

Needing Dr. Stein to finish his story, Adam answered, "So, you were the boy's therapist then?"

Stein blinked several times, and then frowned; looking

at Adam as though he'd said something ridiculous. "I was their father," he informed. "Ruth was my wife. And the one and only time she ever drew me into the dramatics of the boy's school life I turned her down. I was busy. I was being honored for something I don't even recall now and I was unhappy that she'd not be attending with me, so I punished her by refusing to support her in what *she* needed."

A shock of adrenaline pulsed through Adam's body at the revelation. He backtracked through his memory. Adam knew he'd filtered the entire encounter through his own need to find Stein guilty with regard to what he did to children. No family photos anywhere. No holiday decoration. No joy whatsoever filled this home. Still, not everything added up.

"What happened to Ruth, Dr. Stein? Where is your wife?" Adam asked.

Dr. Stein's eyes glazed over and filled with tears as he rubbed slowly at his chest. "Dead." He paused a moment, the hand still over his heart, before looking directly at Adam, focused, accusing. "Surely, you've heard of the *Bay Shadow Killer*?"

Adam adjusted in his seat, sitting forward with interest. "I'm not from here. I've only been in New York a few months. The dreams only started a few weeks ago. Until then, I had no reason to inquire about you." Other than some cursory inquires about the doctor's practice, he'd not been concerned with the man's history. A pang of guilt hit his stomach. He'd followed a ghost, certain the ghost was looking for justice and to save his brother. Instead of questioning everything, he questioned only those things that would help him confirm what he wished to believe. Still, he had to see it to the end. Find the truth and help the dead boy. Scratch at the itch in the back of his mind that said something was off in what Stein had told him. "Tell me what happened."

Stein nodded, grabbed his flask and fortified himself with a long, deep drink. "The teacher, his name was Thomas Voller, he was in charge of mentally ill patients for the 3rd and 4th grades. There was one other teacher in a different classroom and one assistant, but Voller had hand-picked the students he would teach himself and that year he'd chose Freddy. Later, it would come out that Voller was molesting the children. At some point Albert had come to see Freddy and Voller felt certain Albert had seen him with one of the little girls. Of course, Albert hadn't, or he'd have reported it immediately, but Voller wasn't sure, so he ordered Albert to stay away.

"It made Albert suspicious and he began questioning Freddy. When Freddy got upset, Albert went to the principal's office and reported his suspicions. The school tried to cover it up, but the secretary testified later and the principal was fired for warning Voller to stop instead of having him arrested. And later Voller called Ruth to arrange for a late meeting at parent-teacher night, which happened that time every year. Albert insisted he go to the meeting as well. The last meeting of the night."

Adam felt his stomach clench and he swallowed hard, wishing once more for his own flask. He noted how pale Stein had become. The man continued massaging his chest, an action Adam now recognized as soothing his grief, his broken heart. Guilt shamed Adam, but he'd promised Albert he'd help. But, now, something Albert said gave him pause and he tried to bring the details forward. Something didn't quite add up still. He needed time to think it over, but he also needed more information, so he encouraged Stein to continue.

"Did your wife keep her appointment then?" Adam asked, realizing she must have, but needing Stein to get to the end of the story about what happened with the boys.

"They found chloroform had been stolen from the

science lab and some had spilled on rags in the closet in Voller's room. Voller didn't clean up as well as he'd hoped and they found blood on the legs of some of the student desks. Ruth's blood, and Albert's. Later they found the baseball bat he'd used on them put away in the gym equipment room. Also, not as clean as he'd hoped."

"What of the bodies?" Adam asked. "And what did he do with Frederick?"

"He took them all out to Marine Park late that night. Tried setting Ruth and Albert on fire," Stein's voice grew high-pitched as he pushed his fist at his mouth to stop the escaping sob. "Some guys saw the flames and ran in to help. Voller left Ruth burning, Albert's body next to her, and he grabbed Frederick who the guys said was alive at the time."

"The men didn't chase after him?" Adam couldn't suppress his anger. "They let Voller take your son?"

"They thought he'd shot Ruth and Albert. That he had a gun. They put the flames out and called the police. And they'd seen his face." Stein composed himself, his eyes still wet, but his voice under his command. "Voller stashed Frederick and went back to the school to make sure he'd left nothing behind. But, Ruth was never late so I'd called the police by that time. The police put it all together and arrested Voller."

"What about Frederick, then?"

"I wasn't going to let Voller get his hands on Frederick again, so I joined the search party, but I went earlier than everyone else. And I found him. In a marsh area. But, I'd lost my wife, my son, they were all dead." Stein drained the flask setting it hard on his desk. It tipped, but there was nothing to spill out, still he stared at it. "Wild dogs had gotten to Frederick and I got there just in time. Beat them with a walking stick I'd brought with me." He sighed loudly, looking longingly at the flask. "I brought him home."

"But you never told anyone?" Adam.

"They'd have taken him from me," Stein argued, but without much passion. "I'm not a fit parent to raise a boy like Frederick on my own."

"What about his wounds from the wild dogs? And the police?" Adam asked. Giggling came from above, but this time it caught Stein's interest and Adam had to ask again in order to gain the man's attention. "Dr. Stein? Frederick's wounds? The police?"

Stein blinked hard and leaned back in the chair as though exhausted. "I took care of everything, of course. I have the training. The material. And when the police came they just told me Voller had confessed but they'd not been able to locate Frederick. They suspected that he ended up in the water. They searched there, but of course…nothing."

Whispering voices and quiet laughter brought Stein to his feet and he was pulled to the stairs and up to the door above as though there were a magnet that called to souls. Adam followed him, remaining just a few feet behind, allowing Stein time to adjust to hearing the sound of Albert's laughter.

Adam hadn't heard Albert laugh in his dreams, only his mournful and quiet voice asking Adam to bring his brother home. Adam stopped as Stein opened the door, cold fingers of air reaching out to caress them both as the door swung open.

It struck Adam in that moment. What didn't add up. It was 1982. Stein said the boys were born in the late 1960's. The voices were of young boys, but Frederick had to be at least in his early teens by now.

As Stein crossed the threshold Bella barked at an open window with billowing curtains. The window slammed shut as they entered and the laughter stopped. Bella barked at the closed window, and then walked over to Frederick who sat in a rocking chair nearby, a small red ball in his hand. She nosed the boy's hand, stepped back and wagged her tail.

Adam walked around Stein who stood in the center of the room staring at the closed window. The room was cold and he could see Stein and Bella breathing out warm air, Bella's fast and shallow from playing and Stein's long and slow as he considered Albert's abrupt departure.

Adam came to the boy and knelt down to be more on eye-level with him. Icy fingers crawled up Adam's spine as he took the red ball gently from the dead boy's hand. Stein had done extensive work on Frederick's face where the dogs had marred his flesh. The eyes weren't quite right, but they seemed a high quality glass. The doctor had been able to get a smile on the face, but the last few years, or perhaps from a lack of the right material to fully realize a human subject, the color wasn't quite right and some of the skin on the face sagged around the eyes. The doctor's taxidermy skills on the birds Adam had seen throughout the house showed a true talent, but something this large was extremely difficult to keep lifelike.

Stein walked up next to him and put his hand out. Adam looked up, handed the man the red ball and stood.

"I didn't know he had a red ball," Stein said in a nearly monotone voice as he examined the orb.

"I'm sorry for your loss," Adam replied, the hollow feelings of inadequacy opened his heart so cold guilt could fill it. In all of Adam's existence he'd been judged without ever being asked about who he was, what he was, what he was doing, no questions at all. People judged him in silence, walking by quickly to get far away, not making eye contact, or speaking angrily or in fear under their breath as they walked by. And he'd felt the injustice of it, but it hadn't kept him from doing the same to Dr. Stein. "I'm sorry."

Stein hadn't noticed Adam's apology. He continued

looking lovingly at his dead son. "I told you they were close," he said, rubbing absently at his broken heart. "Far more alike now than they ever were in life."

"How have you kept this hidden for so long?" Adam asked, curious how a man could do such a thing but still function in society as though he had no tragic history to contend with.

"My practice had been in Manhattan. I came to Brooklyn. Made sense, since I live here. I fired the entire staff. Broke off with those who would pity me. Those who would remind me by their sheer existence that I had once had a different life. In a single act of selfishness, I let my family be murdered. I left them alone, unprotected, because I had better things to do." The man's voice cracked and Adam watched a tear fall from his face to land on the dead boy's knee.

"You must realize it is time to let him go," Adam said, resting his hand gently on David Stein's shoulder. When Stein didn't reject the touch Adam continued speaking. "Albert sought me out to bring his brother home. And I need your help to reunite the brothers. Tell me, Dr. Stein, where is *home*?"

"If you take him, I will be alone." Stein's voice carried pain that Adam understood completely. "I left my friends behind. Was cold to my family until they finally gave up. I couldn't have visitors, you see."

If it hadn't been for Albert insisting that Frederick be brought home, Adam would have left the doctor and never returned. But, Frederick's brother wouldn't rest until the boys were reunited. Adam could only guess at why Albert had reached out after all these years. Perhaps the boy was looking for the right person to communicate with. Though, admittedly, Adam had never considered himself one that commonly communicates with the dead.

"Believe me when I say that I understand," Adam

offered. "But, it's time. He must rejoin his brother and mother. You've had him long enough."

Stein smirked, but his voice was still full of grief when he spoke. "Spoken like someone who's never had a child." He put the ball back in Frederick's hand and sighed deeply, glancing at the closed window. "But, I suppose you're right. I shouldn't keep the boys apart if they want to be together." He turned to Adam, cheeks wet, defeated by grief. "His home is at Green Wood. I can draw you a map, the place is huge. But, I can't go with you."

"Of course not, I didn't expect you to." Adam agreed. "Would you like me to leave Bella with you? Just until I get back?"

Stein looked at the red ball and smiled. "Both the boys seem to enjoy your little dog, Mr. Frank. I think I might enjoy the company."

Bella wagged her tail, no sign that the doctor was lying about being happy for the company.

"I'm going to have Bella go with you downstairs. I'll need your car keys, a blanket to wrap him in and whatever tools you have on hand."

Stein nodded. "I have what you need." He turned, but hesitated and said, "The boys share a headstone. When they didn't find Frederick's body they assumed he was dead and we put their names together. Is it possible to keep them together? You know, when you return Frederick home."

"Of course, Dr. Stein," Adam answered. "Now, why don't you go downstairs and make some tea. Leave your keys out for me. I'll find my way to your garage for tools."

Stein nodded and followed Bella downstairs without a backward glance.

DAWN BROKE THE NIGHT sky with ribbons of yellow and pink just as Adam pulled into Dr. Stein's garage. The frozen ground had complicated things, but Adam was resourceful and found the equipment he needed to get the job done.

The garage door closed behind him and he got out, putting away the tools he'd taken, making sure they were clean. It was silent inside, which he expected and he took his time even when he went into the house. A detour to the restroom to clean up had him looking at his reflection in a mirror, chastising himself as he'd done all night, for judging Dr. Stein so harshly.

Adam assumed the boys were happy to be reunited, but neither had come to thank him. The cemetery was quiet and not even the dead came out in the cold to watch him. At least none that made themselves known to him.

The sound of scratching at the bathroom door had him drying his hands quickly and he opened it. Bella stood there, a single bark, shrill and urgent had him following her upstairs to a room he'd not entered before. Next to Frederick's room he found Dr. Stein lying fully clothed on his bed, hand over his heart as though he'd been rubbing it. His eyes were open, but he appeared calm even in death.

"I'm glad you were here, my friend," Adam said, petting Bella's head once she'd jumped up on the bed with Dr. Stein. "No one wants to die alone." Adam noted the red ball still in the man's hand.

Adam called the police, telling them the doctor hadn't kept his appointment and asked someone to check on him.

"Let's go Bella," Adam said and she jumped from the bed and preceded him down the stairs. "I think Dr. Stein's heart couldn't take the thought of being alone." He mused out loud, and Bella turned in the hallway as though she were interested in what he was saying. "Now he's not."

Walking out into the new day, air filtered by snow, clean and cold, Adam took a lungful of air and pulled his collar up, more to hide his disfigured face than to stem the cold. Bella pranced at his feet, happy he'd been unable to find her sweater. A cab turned down the street and Adam whistled, throwing his hand up. The cab banked toward the sidewalk, slowing, but as Adam approached the driver's eyes grew large and he quickly turned back onto the street. Adam watched the cab turn the corner and out of sight.

"Dr. Stein did say I could borrow his car." Adam turned back to the house, whistled for Bella and went inside, where the dead were more welcoming than the living. And more helpful.

# The End

# Adam Frankenstein, U.S. Marshal

# Author's Note

I WOULD LIKE TO thank James F. a narcotics detective in the state of Texas and Daniel W. an attorney who works for a federal judge. They were extremely helpful in answering questions about how a warrant works, how anonymous tips are handled and for giving their time freely so my story has some reality to it.

# Dedication

*To my best friend Domini Walker who loves dogs, good suspense novels and sarcasm. Likely, in that order. Marshal Rebecca Hughes is certainly my idea of what you'd be like as a U.S. Marshal; serious about her job, sassy, sarcastic and willing to shoot someone to save a dog.*

# Chapter 1

EATH HAD COME AFTER all these years and this time, he'd not be cheated. Adam felt his spirit rise against the onslaught of rain pouring from the sky, coming to wash away sins and finding them stains. The tears of God did not fall for him, he was certain. No one, not even the Almighty would grieve for him.

Blood pooled beneath him, warm against cold skin. Adam could see it all from his ever-ascending spirit. Body, rattled with bullet holes, blood stains spreading like death's virus from his body to darken the long black duster jacket he wore this time of year. Black Stetson several feet away vibrated and danced along the pool of rushing water rivulets newly made in the violent storm. His favorite hat, a gift from a colleague, a woman who'd once called him handsome though he knew he was anything but, was crushed in the back, the result of a blow to his head with a spike-covered baseball bat.

The sun kissed the clouds gently casting hues of gold, orange and pink across the gray morning sky. Warmth spread across the hay field on the far side of the narrow, paved road and made a path across his sprawled, wet body as it moved into the field nearest him, one decorated with apple trees and swaying shadows.

Adam's ascension slowed as the realization that he felt the warmth across his body signaled the potential of decision.

"Shit." His disembodied voice echoed in his mind. "Exactly how dead am I?"

No great voice from the sky answered. No devil laughed with glee. He was an anomaly even in death. The warmth spread as the sun's rays fattened with the promise of a new day and the storm slowed in defeat.

"No pain," Adam thought. Looking at his contorted body, face up, one leg straight, the other bent, head slightly turned toward the apple trees, he realized something about himself that he'd only speculated on previously. "Damn, I'm one big, ugly bastard." Six foot six wasn't a giant, but it was notable. In the 19th century it had been more a curse, but no more than the scars that disfigured his face and limbs.

As the light shone down on his body his thoughts struggled to escape the haze of his dying mind. A dull ache in the region of his skull threatened and fingers like ice whispered across his spirit, pulling him up, nearer the end of his immortality. Nearer to judgment. If there was anything to fear it was that there really was a God, and that Adam Frankenstein would be held accountable for everything he'd done in his two centuries on this earth. The ache grew and a burn made of ice moved down his spine.

"Take me," he whispered without speaking. "I'm done. There's nothing more I can do to atone. Judge me. What do I have to lose? Other than a life full of purpose, but not love, colleagues but not friends. What greater Hell could be waiting for me?"

Those cold fingers pulled at him once more. The ache grew and those fingers dug in. Torn, his mind held to his spirit, which was still tethered to his broken body and as he realized what secured him, what refused to release him into the unknown, his left side and lower abdomen sparked with pain as a name ripped his spirit from the grasp of death.

"Bella."

# CHAPTER 2

BELLA WATCHED SEVERAL MEN in stained wife-beaters moving crates from the back of a large white van and heard the cries of fear and despair. The sun shone through the struggling raindrops, the spoils of war nothing more than thick humid air. She knew this place. She and Adam spent most of the night staking out the compound made of a semicircle of single-wide trailers that housed one caretaker, with the rest filled with the crates.

Looking through the bars of her prison pain brought her breath in quick and shallow. The pain would pass, but the fear for what these bastards had done to Adam pushed the boundaries of her courage and caused tears to gather and burn. She was the only one who knew Adam had been captured. She had no way to contact the field office, or Marshal Hughes. Anyone else who would help Adam lived too far away. She and Adam had lived in Texas for six months, but Adam had a difficult time making friends. If it weren't for her, for their friendship, he'd have been the most solitary creature she'd ever come across. Now she was imprisoned, he'd been taken away bloody and the question of exactly how immortal they both were was going to be put to the test. No one was coming to save them. They still had only each other.

Two men broke from the others at the van and walked

toward her. The rain did nothing to dampen the smell of tobacco, sweat and evil that clung to their skin. Bella backed away as far as her prison would allow when they stopped in front of her, gazing in like she was some kind of freak.

"She sure can take a beating." The man who spoke appeared to be in charge. The others followed his orders without question. Cracked lips pulled back in a smirk revealing stained and rotting teeth. "Heard she bit Keeper pretty good. Give her a day and let's see what she can do."

The other man's head moved up and down with vigor like a bobble head on the dashboard in stop and go traffic. She didn't know this man's name, but the leader, they called him JC, and if she were able to get out of her prison he'd be the first one to lose his balls.

The smell of kerosene, blood and wood smoke announced the arrival of the injured Keeper right before he came into view from her left. Bella's hackles went up and the growl that escaped without thought came from deep inside her soul.

"You're not going to keep this damn dog are you? Just throw her to one of the big dogs." Keeper rubbed his bandaged right hand and spat at her. "She has to be near dead anyway. No good for fighting. No good as bait. Maybe Brutus would eat her. He eats cats." Keeper leaned forward; likely emboldened by her incarceration and his belief she was near death.

Bella rushed the cage door, her paw reaching through to scratch the man's face, nearly taking an eye. The howl of pain brought laughter from the other two as Keeper's hand came away with blood staining the bandage from their previous encounter.

"You bitch!" Keeper pulled out a gun, but JC knocked it down before it could be aimed.

"Look at her." JC pushed the man back a step. "She's

covered in blood, but she doesn't act as though she's wounded. Tough dog. And you know our clientele love it when we pit the smaller dogs against the big ones. She can't be more than fifteen, maybe sixteen pounds. She could make us a lot of money."

"Yeah, some breed of MinPin is my guess, but I've never seen a merle-colored one before. I will say, if they know this is that new marshal's dog, it could be a main event fight. That man's made more enemies in a few months than I have my whole damned life." The man with JC peered in at her, but didn't try to get close. "I'll get her back to health. JC's right. This one's a money maker." He laughed as Bella growled. "She's a tough one, I'll give you that. Small, but tough."

JC nodded. "Keeper, you stay clear of this dog. She'd got it out for you and I don't want her damaged any further. Let Cam here fix her up." When Keeper didn't answer JC struck out with his index finger hitting the man hard in the throat. Keeper cried out and stumbled back, but nodded. "You touch that dog, *anyone* touches that dog, and they'll answer to me."

"Don't sweat it, JC," Cam said. "I'll keep her with me. She bit more than just Keeper. And not all of the men can control their temper."

The world shifted for a moment as Cam lifted her crate. She considered lashing out at him, but thought better of it. She needed someone to like her. Someone to feed her and keep her safe. Someone to trust her enough to let her out. Cam looked just stupid enough to be that someone.

# Chapter 3

Drawing in air Adam thought his lungs might burst. Pain rushed in on the exhale, his body shaking violently, uncontrollably. This wasn't the first time he'd sustained such wounds, but he'd not had his head crushed in, his heart pierced by lead and nearly drained from blood loss all at once. He'd had those things happen throughout the years, just not together.

His body had divorced his free will so he lay there in the middle of the road breathing in the humid air, tasting the tang of oil, gas and asphalt on his tongue each time he pulled in oxygen, a coppery aftertaste chaser that was his own blood. He knew where he was, but not how he got there. Assumingly, those backwoods bastards dumped him close to his home, which unfortunately was out in the middle of nowhere.

"Bella?" The yell barely sounded a whisper and ended on a long, painful cough. An attempt to raise his head proved to be futile so he tried moving his limbs. "Jesus!" The bent leg straightened bringing to life lower back pain that rivaled his headache. Damage like this would take time to heal. "Bella." Apprehension flowed like ice from his heart through his body.

Tires on wet asphalt swooshed in the distance, a car engine purring closer at an alarming pace. "Son of a bitch." Adam pushed past the screaming pain that had shackled him to the ground and rolled to one side as he pushed with both hands. Swaying, the world spinning, he concentrated on remaining upright, his knees protesting until he leaned back to rest his ass on his heels. A quick audit of his faculties forced him to his feet. This close to death, he wasn't sure what he could do if they'd come back to make sure he was dead. But, someone would tell him what happened to Bella before the Reaper got his due.

Patting his hip he pushed the heavy duster aside, hope and anger mixing a heady brew of righteousness and pissed-off as he pulled the Glock from its holster. Squeezing his eyes shut to clear them he opened them again, but the approaching car was still a black blur. Stumbling two steps to the right he steadied himself once more pulling air through clenched teeth as he took aim. The black spot grew larger, but the vehicle slowed and Adam was finally able to make out the telltale outline of a government car. Blinking hard he lowered his gun when the car stopped ten feet from him and the door opened.

"My God, Adam, what the hell's happened to you?"

Relief washed through him at the familiar feminine voice. "Marshal Hughes, I can't find my dog."

He nearly collapsed when she put her arm around him, taking some of his weight on her small frame. The top of her head wasn't any higher than his shoulders, but she was strong. She leaned into him, pulling him closer to her, then walked him to the car, turned him around and sat him against the hood. He sat, metal popping in complaint. She moved in front of him, her legs against his to help him remain in place as she pulled her cell out. She stabbed at the numbers, then frowned.

"No reception out here, Adam," she explained. Her gaze took in the area, scanning. "You just had to live out in the middle of nowhere. How bad are you?" Genuine concern gave a gloss to her eyes and she bit her lip.

"I'll live." He assured her, but knew what she saw, and knew she didn't believe him. "Most of the blood isn't mine," he lied, "But, I'm in pretty bad shape."

"If I step away will you fall?" She asked, scanning the area once more.

"No."

She backed up slowly, her intelligent blue eyes looking him over like he was a walking crime scene. He was a crime scene, just not a walking one at the moment. Seemingly satisfied that he'd not fall on his face she turned away. Walking fifty feet north of the car she started calling for Bella. When there was no sign of the dog she walked fifty feet south of the car, carefully checking both sides of the road. At one point she bent over to retrieve his Stetson, examined it closely and looked at him for several seconds before continuing her search.

Watching her check the ditch for Bella caused Adam's heart to beat fast and bile to climb up his throat. If she'd been broken, like him, perhaps she couldn't call out to him, couldn't move, but she could heal faster than he could. She wasn't there.

"Hughes! We need to get to my home. Now." He pushed away from the hood, flinching at the pain. He fell back against the hood. "Rebecca!" he shouted, his voice no longer weak. Already healing, it would still be days before he was back to normal. Bella was with the men who ran the state's largest dog fighting ring. Dangerous men who would throw her into a pit to be ripped apart. And Bella was immortal. When she didn't die, how many times would they put her in the pit?

Rebecca was there, pulling him to his feet, walking him to the passenger side where the door was open and waiting. He gritted his teeth as he pulled his legs in and adjusted in the seat. The door slammed and in seconds she was in the car, reaching for the radio. He grabbed her hand, rough, smearing blood across her knuckles. She froze and he realized he was hurting her. He let go and their eyes met.

"If you call for help they'll want me to go to the hospital and I can't do that." Adam wanted to trust her. He liked her. She was good at her job, loyal, tough. She'd seen him do things, things most men could never do. When he explained that he had always been strong and agile she let it drop and he figured she pegged him as a steroid user. She'd seen other things, too, and she'd never told anyone else. Now, he was going to have to tell her things that he couldn't explain away so easily.

"Adam, you need to go to the hospital," she said, a note of desperation moving from her words to her eyes. "I'll find her. I promise you. I'll do nothing else until I find her."

"I believe you," he said as he sat back. "But, these men are dangerous, some of them ex-military. A lot of money at stake. They'll be on alert, worried about a bust. As we speak they're likely changing the location of tonight's fight. I need to get to their base of operations and get someone there to give me the location. I can't wait for a warrant."

The car rolled away in the direction of his house. Rebecca Hughes, a decorated marshal, said nothing for several minutes and the silence gave Adam time to reflect on how he'd ended up beaten nearly to death and left in the middle of the road.

The man who ran the dog fights was JC Milton. Milton's cousin was Warren Milton, who had a fondness for girls not yet in high school. Warren had escaped custody and Adam was told JC was likely to give him refuge. JC was a drug dealer, but when Adam discovered he also ran the dog fights, he wasn't going to simply go in and retrieve

Warren, he was going to shut down JC and his cronies. But, there wasn't a warrant for JC and an initial search of the man's property gave no indication Warren had been there. So, Adam started at one end of the Milton's fifty acres and systematically combed the woods for a hide out. Rebecca told him he'd have to get solid proof that there was another house on the property in order for her to get the search warrant. When he didn't tell her how he planned on getting that proof, she'd dropped it with a simple, "It has to stand up in court."

"That's a lot of blood on your clothes, Adam." She broke the silence, handing him his hat. "And there's no way you could've been wearing that hat when all that damage was done to it. So what? They threatened your hat with violence to get you to go away? What the hell happened?"

"I told you, most of this blood isn't mine," he insisted. "I was attacked from behind and one of them took my hat. Unfortunately for him, he was wearing it when I attacked back." Lying was normally a smooth tool, but something about the fact that she had his back, was loyal and had even attempted friendship caused the lie to stick in his throat and he hesitated before rushing back to assure her. "It's possible that I killed a couple of them. They must have knocked me out, thought I was dead and dropped me as close to my house as they were willing to go. For all they knew, I have someone waiting for me at home. Can't take a chance at being seen."

"Or, maybe they had second thoughts about killing a U.S. Marshal and left you close enough to walk home? If we get back up, we can bring them in and ask them about it. If we don't..." she let the words linger, both of them knowing they could get into a lot of trouble if they didn't report this.

"Believe me," Adam sat straighter, his mind beginning to clear as the pain receded. "they left me for dead."

"So this is revenge? I can't go along with that. I get wanting to save your dog, I really do. But, you must realize they've likely already killed her. I can't imagine *your* dog going down without a fight if a bunch of thugs were beating the shit out of you."

"Bella is alive," he said with confidence. "And I'm going to go home, clean up and grab a few things I'll need to save her."

"If you can promise that we'll go in, save Bella and not kill anyone, I'll help you." She didn't look at him, but pulled off onto a side road that took them down a gravel road canopied by tree limbs nearly bare of their leaves.

"I don't want you going with me." He winced as the car stopped abruptly a few feet from his front door. Tension was as heavy as the humidity. "If this goes sideways, I don't want you in trouble. I'm pretty certain Warren Milton is going to be at those fights. He must know by now what they did to me. This is his chance at a little freedom while they all think I'm dead or in the hospital. If I'm right, I'll say I followed him in and if I'm wrong, you don't want to be there. No use both of us losing our jobs."

Rebecca slammed the door and came to help him out. They struggled to get to the front door, dizziness causing him to stagger, nearly taking them both down twice before they got to the door. He was healing, but the blow to the head was significant and vertigo made walking a challenge.

She propped him against the door jam and unceremoniously shoved her hand deep into his front, right pocket. Removing his keys she opened his front door and they staggered inside where she put him on the couch. Looking down at her white blouse she pursed her lips.

"This shirt is ruined," she claimed. "I suppose you don't have any women's clothes on hand here?"

Adam stood, removed his jacket letting it fall to the

wood floor. He needed to move, to get dressed, get armed and get back to where they might still have Bella in their home base. His fingers felt stiff as he began unbuttoning his shirt.

"No," he answered, "but you're welcome to borrow one of mine." His shirt joined the coat on the floor and he moved in the direction of his bedroom. Ice filled his veins as he considered what Bella was going through at that very moment.

"Adam." Her voice held such shock he turned to ensure there were no intruders, but found only her, standing there, eyes wide as she stared at him.

He knew immediately what the problem was and he didn't have time for it. But, if it won her cooperation, he'd give her the short version.

"I've fought in many wars," he said as he turned to face her, not wanting her to examine the tattoo that took up most of his back. A tattoo that would only result in more questions. "I've been near bombs when they detonated, took shrapnel, my body used as a human shield, cut, shot, you name it. This is the result." He stood tall, allowing her to take in the scars, hoping she'd not ask about the discoloration of skin between his extremities and torso. That she'd not ask how he could possibly have survived some of the scars.

The tears gathering in her eyes dried as she nodded. Whatever it was that gave her courage, that made her tough, filtered through her iron will and she tucked it all away. As he waited to see if she'd ask more questions he watched a light blush rise from her neck, settling in her cheeks.

"Maybe you should get dressed," she suggested as she turned her attention to the window.

She was an enigma. She fought like a man, shot like a man, talked like a man when they were working, but she'd blushed at seeing him without a shirt. She was always so in control, so strong-willed, sometimes he discounted her more feminine side. It was ungentlemanly to do so and he made a note to be more thoughtful as he moved to ready himself.

The water was as hot as he could stand it and as it cascaded down his back he contemplated his next move. Letting the warmth wash the blood away he stared at the drain, water pink and dirty, then running clean. Everything was about moving forward. Looking back was a well of regret that could be maddening. Rebecca would call for back-up, or she wouldn't. She would help, or she wouldn't. Bella had been his only true friend for over a century. She'd followed him into wars, to seek justice, to find answers, anywhere without a hint of hesitancy. He'd found some friends along the way, but Bella's loyalty, her love, was constant and unconditional.

Turning off the water he pulled back the shower curtain and grabbed the towel on the counter. Blood still trickled from some of the wounds, those that hit arteries or major organs, but other wounds had already begun to heal. Drying off he swiped the large mirror with the damp towel and looked back at his haggard face. A face less frightening today than it had been in the days where freaks were only accepted in carnivals, or killed. The scar that ran from just inside his hairline on the left to the bottom of his jaw on the same side bisected his eye, leaving half blue and half amber. In another life he'd been handsome. A strong man in a circus until the lions ripped away a leg, an arm and a hand. And destroyed his face. Simple enough to reattach, insane enough to reanimate. His maker found fairly suitable substitutes. But, those scars would never heal.

The ache in his head throbbed in echo down his neck making it difficult to turn very far in either direction. Dressing took longer than he'd hoped, but he knew exactly what weapons he'd take and those were always easy to access, and plentiful. Emerging back into the living room he was packing two Glocks, several knives, a collapsible bow staff and a hand grenade.

Rebecca sat at the table in the kitchen area, one of his black t-shirts cut short and tied in a knot to one side in order to fit her smaller frame. She held the Stetson in one hand, examining the holes and tears in the back. He'd never seen her dressed in anything but her suit, their friendship fenced inside the framework of professionalism. She'd given him the Stetson as a 'welcome to Texas' gift and he'd grown fond of the thing. Now he'd give anything to be rid of it.

"The amount of blood on this," she turned the ruined back toward him and poked one her fingers through a hole, "someone's dead. No one could survive this kind of damage."

"If someone died, I know nothing of it." The woman was like a human lie detector, much like Bella, so sticking as close to the truth as possible was the safe bet. "What I do know is that we need to go." He'd put on another long jacket, this time the black leather one he wore when he moved here from New Orleans. It hid some of the weapons, but was surprisingly light-weight making it easy to reach his weapons. "Are you coming?" He gently took the hat and set it on the table. Her eyes followed it, then ran up his arm to meet his gaze.

"I know you're strong as hell, Adam, but I think you're hurt more than you claim." She stood, her hand fell lightly to his chest, moved down a few inches and in a flash she pushed hard.

He winced as he stepped back. "Dammit, Rebecca." A dark stain blossomed, turning a spot on his dark blue shirt black.

Her hands rested on her hips. "Sit down." She moved her eyes to the chair next to where she'd been sitting.

"We don't have time for this."

"You want my cooperation? My help?" She pointed one long, well-manicured finger at the chair. "Sit."

If Adam had learned anything since moving here it was that you didn't argue with a Texas woman. He sat, frowning at her in defiance. He'd just leave, but the world kept spinning anytime he moved too fast. He needed her. He couldn't take a chance of going back for Bella and not walking out with her. They'd know how important she was and they'd know something wasn't entirely copasetic with him. They'd double their efforts to kill him, or use Bella against him. He needed to hit them hard, quick and with an element of surprise. That wasn't going to happen if he was staggering around.

Rebecca stood in front of him looking him up and down, then slowly walked around to the back of the chair. He remained still, worry creeping in like vines around his chest, causing him to breathe in slow, shallow breaths.

Her fingers were cool against the heat of his neck. Something inside his gut knotted as she ran her index finger across new wounds freshly healed, or healing. As she slid two fingers up the nape of his neck and into his hair.

Sucking air through clenched teeth he whispered, "Stop." Neither of them moved for several moments, her fingers light on his tender scalp.

She stepped back into view, taking her seat and looking at scant blood on her fingertips. She grabbed the material left from when she'd cut the bottom of his t-shirt off and wiped them clean. First she stared at the material discarded on the table. Adam felt his gut clench. He wanted to give her time, but he didn't have much to give.

"Last month, when we were chasing the Cortes cousins," she began, her eyes still trained on the table, "Jorge was afraid to get in the car with you. Horrified, actually. At first I thought it was because he'd taken a swipe at you with that big-ass blade of his and he knew assaulting an officer of the law was going to make things twice as hard on him. You'd bled a lot, but we got to the station and you seemed fine. Wouldn't even go to the hospital."

Adam remained silent as he watched her pick up the Stetson and push her index finger through one of the holes again.

"If I put this hat on you, will these holes line up with those wounds?" She cut her eyes to him, pinning him with her sharp gaze.

He held his eyes on hers, that feeling in the pit of his stomach coiling till it turned to ice. Other people knew his real identity. Not many, but a few. They'd accepted him. Of course, they weren't entirely human either, so it was easier to accept. Rebecca wasn't exactly by-the-book, but she was no-nonsense and what he had to share would certainly *not* make sense. But, he owed her respect and that meant not bullshitting her.

"Yes."

"Was Jorge right to be terrified of you that night?

"He had reason."

She swallowed hard as she put the hat back down. "Those are big holes in that hat." When he said nothing she continued, "It's ripped too, so not bullet holes. Something with spikes?" Again he said nothing. "Swung hard. Holes that big, they went deep." It wasn't a question, but he answered.

"Yes."

"What are you, Adam? Some kind of X-man? Military experiment?" Before he could speak she put her hand up, palm toward his face. "Don't you dare tell me you're a vampire. Even I have my limits on what I'll believe."

"So you'd believe I'm an X-man, but not a vampire?" He couldn't stop the twitch at the corner of his mouth threatening a smile.

The sun moved pushing rays of light through the window, highlighting the gold streaks in her hair. He noticed, for the first time, that the kitchen smelled of fresh brewed coffee. She didn't have a cup yet, so he got one for her, and himself, poured the dark liquid, handing her a cup as he sat back down with him.

"Some kind of genetic enhancement or mistake, I could believe that. A hiccup in the evolutional chain giving you a physical advantage. You know, something science can explain. Not some myth."

He sipped his coffee, considering his words. "Rebecca, you're not going to like this."

# Chapter 4

I

F YOU BITE ME, THINGS will go bad for you dog. I don't care what JC says." Cam pulled Bella's crate from the back of his beat up Ford pick-up and walked toward a doublewide trailer propped off the ground with gray cinderblocks.

The day had grown hotter and the humidity refused to give up without a fight. The drive from where she and Adam had been jumped to this new place was the only good thing to happen to her in the last 24 hours. Hers was a wire crate and the back of the truck was uncovered, so the air cooled her down. It was *clean* air, not filled with rancid breath, sour body odor and smoke. And blood.

Each intake of breath brought pain to her ribs that radiated through her chest. Being unable to die didn't keep the pain away. One more day and the pain would be less, perhaps gone altogether. History had taught her that time heals all wounds. She licked at her front paw where her dewclaw had been ripped off. The soothing motion was stopped abruptly as Cam sat her crate down hard on the porch, jarring it until the pain in her ribs escaped on a cry she couldn't stop. The subsequent growl was low and came without thought.

"You better watch your manners," he warned as he fished out his keys and opened the door.

Urine, feces and fear mixed with the clinging smell of marijuana and alcohol as she was carried over the threshold. Cam kicked the door closed behind them, flicking on a light and illuminating a living area so dirty Bella cringed. She looked for an exit door, but only saw three windows, all closed except the one near the door which was propped open so a box fan could fit in it. For a moment she was relieved as they quickly passed through the living area when she was taken down the hall to a closed door. Someone had left a hole in the door that hadn't gone all the way through, but the smells seeped from the crack at the bottom causing Bella to release a suppressed whine of fear and disgust. She knew those smells. Places that smelled like that were filled with the wounded and the nearly dead.

Walking in, her senses were assaulted with a concentration of such vile odors she coughed and hid her nose beneath her paws, but kept her eyes scanning the area. The far wall, near the only window in the small room, were stacks of wire kennels similar to the ones she was in. Each was occupied, six dogs in all, not counting her. Two stood, tails wagging like idiots and Bella felt overwhelmed with nausea. Unlike her, they were simple dogs. Beaten, abused, betrayed, they still stood, hopeful someone would show them affection.

"Hey Bono! Hey Czar! How are my boys doing?" Cam's voice belied his evil intent and Bella was amazed that when the man stuck his fingers in the cage that neither dog tried to bite them off.

As he let Czar lick his fingertips he placed her crate directly on top of Bono's, her ribs screaming in pain, but not enough to make her give away how badly she still hurt. It was time to take control of herself despite how little courage she currently felt.

Music began to play and the man brought out his

phone, hit a button and turned away from them. He stopped short as a voice on the other end began talking.

"Bono can be ready in a couple of days. I need to pull his water first. He's a bleeder, so we need to dehydrate him first. Czar needs at least another week." He turned back to the wall of crates, peering into each little prison. "Chopper, Prince and Grim will be two weeks if you want them to win. One if you just want them to last a while for show." He scrunched his nose, frown so deep he suddenly had only one brow, as he crouched at the last crate farthest from Bella. Hitting on the door he shook his head. "Max isn't going to make it. Damn shame. He's lasted the longest of them all. JC is going to be pissed." He stood, turned and walked out of the room, closing the door behind him.

Tears burned behind her lids. She wished fervently she was like the other dogs in this room; incapable of truly understanding just how screwed they all were. Living over a hundred years she'd learned more human words, recognized them, comprehended them. Adam had taught her much, and without him the weight of despair grew cold in her small chest. She needed him and now he had no idea where she was. A tear spilled out and she licked it away.

# Chapter 5

"I'M NOT USUALLY AT a loss for words," Rebecca said calmly, then sipped her coffee. "I know you passed the psych eval, or you'd not have been assigned to the Marshal Service. You are a real Marshal, right?"

"I have real documents that attest to that fact." He wasn't sure how much more she could take. "I have been trained to be a Marshal. And you'll find my work history complete should you look it up online."

"When a person can't say a simple 'yes' or 'no' it usually means they're lying about at least part of it." She sipped the coffee again, holding the cup in both hands. "Six months I've worked with you." She shook her head, took a large drink and choked.

Adam reached out to take the cup and she recoiled.

The knot in his stomach took on more weight and his heart felt the pang of guilt and pain. Having a woman recoil from him was not new. It was natural, at least for him. Always had been. But, in this modern time, where people were desensitized to things that had once shocked men and women a century earlier, people would mostly ignore him, which was an improvement over them trying to kill him on sight. Her reaction was forgivable, understandable and still stung like hell.

As she recovered Adam sat back, drew in a deep breath

and closed his eyes to concentrate. Living a long life of rejection and loneliness gave him a sort of gift; the gift to systematically process his emotions and turn them off at will. He'd stopped looking for friends years ago. It was futile and if he let himself care about the constant rejection, he'd become more a monster than what he'd been born. He opened his eyes, and processed the data they took in as he let the shield of apathy work its magic like armor.

The hat was in her hands once more. "Adam Frank... Adam Frankenstein. I don't know what I can believe about you. But no one walks away from something like this. No normal person."

"I don't have time to convince you, or answer whatever questions you have right now," Adam said as he waited for that click, the one deep inside his soul that shut off feelings he no longer wanted. "You do what you feel you need to. Call for help. Don't call for help. Come with me, stay here, go back to the field office in Houston and pretend you never saw me today." He stood, her eyes trailed him. "But, I'm headed back to that place and I'm getting Bella. I'm shutting them down, however that needs to happen." Vertigo caused the world to tilt and his hands tightened on the back of his chair as he waited for it to pass.

Setting the black Stetson down she stood, pushed her chair in and faced him. "It's obvious that there's something different about you. I don't like feeling made a fool of, Adam, so this best not come back to haunt me. You owe me more of an explanation, but you're right, time is ticking. If you're going in, I'll go with you. But, whatever we do, when we bring these guys down, it has to stick. So you best have a plan."

Trees just outside the kitchen window began to dance in the wind throwing shades across her face; dark then light. The t-shirt she'd cut up sagged at the shoulders giving the impression she was smaller than she really was, starved perhaps. But, her hair and make-up were well done, her trousers from an upscale store were clean and she smelled faintly of strawberries and cream. He knew she'd been a soldier, deployed in some rough places. But, standing there she looked unsure, a touch of fear causing her to bite at her lower lip repeatedly, something he'd seen her do before, teased her about.

"Like I said, I don't want you to come with me. Just finding me and getting me home, that's help enough." Concern for her belied his efforts to remain emotionally detached. He blamed it on his wounds, the lack of blood, exhaustion. "If things go bad, I can take it. You, however..."

"Just stop," she said, her hand tucking a golden strand of hair behind her ear. Drawing in a deep breath she reached into her pants pocket and pulled out a hair tie that she used to put hers in a ponytail. "For six months you've been a pain in my ass with that dog of yours going on every mission. You're lucky I love dogs. You irritate me with your one-finger typing and inability to retain any instruction on how to use the database or fill out reports. You piss me off when you go all Maverick when we're chasing bad guys and they end up with broken bones or lost teeth that we have to explain later." She tightened the knot at the side of the t-shirt and squared her shoulders. "But, for all that you got balls and you're loyal to a fault, so we're going to table this whole Frankenstein thing until I have some bourbon ready."

Adam watched her wordlessly, an involuntary tick in the right side of his jaw had him clenching and unclench-ing it as he contemplated his next move. He didn't want to feel anything about whether she came with him or not. If she came, he had a good chance at covering up any unpleasantness that happened and keeping his job. No one challenged the word of Marshal Rebecca Hughes. If she said something went down a certain way, that's how it happened. He'd only been there for six months. No one was going to believe that it was self-defense if he happened to kill a dozen or so men while trespassing on property he wasn't cleared to be on. Thing was, he did feel something. He felt like shit was about to happen, and not to him this time. And that felt pretty damn good.

# CHAPTER 6

THE ODOR OF MARIJUANA wafted under the door to mix with the rancid sour smell of urine and disinfectant. A single white fan on a tall stand oscillated back and forth giving brief moments of reprieve from the increasing heat. Escape might have to wait for nightfall. By then Bella was certain the pain from her wounds would be gone and she'd be stronger. Cam had left the padlock on her crate, making it impossible to jimmy it open, but none of the other dog crates appeared to be locked, so she would bide her time.

Shuffling brought her attention to the crate farthest from her. Scratches on plastic, paper, a heavy thump and a long sigh ending in a whispered cry brought Bella to the front of her crate, her small, black nose pushing as far out as the bars would allow, scenting past the odors of the room, concentrating on the noisy crate. But, then no sound, not even crying and she pushed harder, sniffed and growled in desperate frustration. A few of the other dogs, closer to the crate, began to whine, following her lead and sticking their noses through the bars.

A blue-gray head flopped against the bars and she could see just enough of the dog Cam had called "Max" to make eye contact. Intelligent gray eyes, heavy lids opening and closing, opening and closing until they focused on the door leading out to the hall. He whined, his nose, as gray as the rest of him, moved between the bars before his eyes closed again.

Movement in the hall had all the dogs moving forward as one by one Bella watched noses peek through each crate. Tails hit metal as they wagged, welcoming their warden as Cam walked in, wiping mustard across his dirty t-shirt, cheeks bulging as he chewed what remained of his food. Bella watched his every move, her heart racing as the door stood ajar.

Shuffling as though he were an old man instead of a lazy asshole, Bella watched Cam open a cupboard. Instead of storage cubbies, a short wooden board came down making a table. Bella realized there were shallow shelves inside the cupboard as Cam reached for a vial of clear liquid. He sat it on the makeshift tabletop and gathered some gauze, a needle and syringe.

Bella's hackles went up as a deep, low growl caught Cam's attention. He cocked his head sideways, studying her before he smiled.

"This ain't for you little girl." His voice was soft and melodious. "This here is for Max. We're going to do him a solid and put him down so he's not suffering." Cam peeled back the plastic, exposing a small syringe with needle attached. Before he could pick up the vial music rang out into the room. "Dammit."

Pulling out his phone he sat the syringe down. "What the hell do you want?"

Bella could hear the voice on the other end. A voice that caused her to bare her teeth. She couldn't make out all the words, but she heard Max's name.

"Well, that's just shitty," Cam yelled into the phone. "Max here has been a good fighter. Never once bit one of us. He earned an easy go, Keeper."

A few more words and Cam ended the call, running

his now-free hand through his oily hair. "Dammit!" He kicked a small metal trash can. It thumped hard against the wood paneling and landed with equal force against the linoleum floor. The metal lid fell open in a gaping scream toward the ceiling. Something inside rattled around, but nothing fell out. Cam snatched it up and put it back in its place.

Walking to Max he crouched down and pet the pit-bull's blue nose. Thumping, methodical and slow caused Cam to smile. "Sorry buddy. You're just too famous to go into that quiet night without some fanfare."

Bella's heart was in a vice of despair. Without a way out she couldn't help Max, couldn't bite Cam, couldn't find Adam. How Max couldn't sense the treachery of the man petting his head and misquoting Dylan Thomas was hard for her to understand. Either of those sins should have won the man a hard bite to a soft spot, but Max just wagged his tail and soaked up the attention.

"Keeper will bring ya some drugs, make you feel bet-ter, stronger. You'll like it," Cam promised as he patted the dog's head, then stood to face Bella. "In the mean-time, let's get you cleaned up little girl. How about a bath? Sound good?"

She forced her hackles down and her tail to wag. Her heart picked up speed as he unlocked her crate.

# Chapter 7

THE GROUND WAS WET and the front of Adam's shirt soaked it up. His elbows rested on wet foliage as he peered through binoculars into the compound where he'd been ambushed.

"All this on JC's land?" Rebecca lay next to him propped up in similar fashion, but she'd put her wind breaker down to keep from getting more wet than necessary.

"Yes."

"How'd you find it? The warrant we got only extended to the house and outbuildings" She pulled her binoculars down and he looked toward her.

"This isn't an outbuilding?" Adam lifted one brow in question.

"That's the thing, Adam. If we had our shit together and some help from headquarters we'd probably be able to find out if that warrant extends to these buildings. All JC has to do is claim they're rentals and we got shit for admissible evidence."

He shrugged because he knew she didn't require a response. She was making a point. Instead he went back to something he could respond to.

"After we didn't find Warren at JC's home I looked up what other property he owns. Not just buildings, but undeveloped land." He propped up on one elbow to better face her, but scanned their vicinity before continuing. "His initial property lines end about a quarter of a mile before a second property begins, which he also owns. Paperwork says there's nothing there, but what are the chances he'd own land so close to home and do nothing with it?"

"Maybe he's just not the industrious kind? Maybe he ran out of money to develop more property? Maybe he was hoping prices in the neighborhood would spike and he could sell for profit?"

"Maybe," he agreed. "And maybe he's a lowlife asshole hoping to hide his criminal activity far from prying eyes? I played the odds. I found this place."

"So, you just went walking around the forest in the dead of night like some..." she stopped, mouth clamping tight, head shaking. "You arbitrarily wandered around his property until you found something that led to this place?"

Wind picked up moving leaves across the forest floor. They both scanned the area before going back to their conversation.

"What were you going to say?" Adam asked. "Walking around in the dead of night like a...what?"

She blushed, causing him to pin her down with his best serious stare, which only caused her to blush more. "Say it."

"I don't want to," she pleaded.

"Say it anyway."

She rolled her eyes heavenward and forced a quick breath out in a rush. "Zombie. Okay? Walking around in the dead of night like a zombie. Happy?"

"That's it? What's wrong with that?"

She shrugged before putting her elbows back down and binoculars back to her eyes. "I was worried it might be offensive."

He looked at her a moment longer, but centuries of

learning and experience left him with only a grunt for an answer and a twitch of a smile.

"Look!" Rebecca pointed to his left. "It's your guy, Warren." Her voice was breathless and filled with excitement. "You know what that means?"

He was already sitting up, his body vibrating with excitement. "Yes. But, you better call in the anonymous tip. They'll never suspect it was you. If I try to disguise my voice I just sound drunk, drugged or stupid."

She was punching numbers on her phone. "Try sounding like a woman. No one would expect that."

He frowned, but was denied a chance to reply when she started talking into the phone, giving directions where they could find Warren Milton, drugs, weapons and a dog fighting ring.

Rebecca hung up and sighed. "It'll take them a while to rally the troops, so we just need to wait it out."

Adam was already back on his belly, sighting Warren Milton with his binoculars and wishing he had his AR 15 and no witnesses. Milton was a special kind of scum who read obituaries and targeted the homes of the widows or widowers. He'd escaped custody while in Louisiana and got onto Adam's radar when someone said he'd been seen at his favorite cousin's house outside of Houston.

"How did you know JC and his crew had him? Milton's reputation?" Rebecca asked just before she received a text. "Headquarters." She punched numbers and someone on the other end picked up immediately.

"Yeah, I know where Adam is," she said. "His phone's on the fritz. We'll need to get him a new one."

As the person on the other end spouted information Rebecca replied, promised to get the information to Adam and hung up.

Adam rolled over, putting the binoculars away. "Now no one from headquarters will be surprised to see us here now." He got up, still crouched low and walked back to Rebecca's vehicle that was out of sight of the compound. She remained close behind him and neither said another word until they were at the car. She threw her wet jacket and binoculars on the trunk and joined him in the car.

She watched him buckle up and sighed loudly into the car. "You have no intention of waiting, do you?"

Ignoring the questions he replied, "I knew Warren was there because I knew JC was lying. And I knew JC was lying because Bella told me."

"What? Don't tell me you have a talking dog." Her eyebrows shot up so high Adam smiled.

"Not exactly," he assured her. "But she comprehends more than a normal dog. A lot more. And she has her own way to communicate with me. We've been together a very long time."

"Uh, okay," she replied. "So how did Bella know?"

A sudden sense of pride took hold of his heart and he sat up straight, turning to look her in the eye.

"Bella can sense lies. It's her gift."

"Her gift?"

"Yes."

"Like a bona fide lie detector?" The brows shot up once more, but this time the corners of her lips twitched as though the thought amused her. "That's some gift."

"It is."

Her brows came down and she cocked her head as though studying him. "Science or magic?"

Adam smiled. "Magic, until someone figures out how it works."

Buzzing vibrated the seat and Rebecca pulled her cell phone from her pocket. Staring at the small screen she said, "Barnes says there's a bit of a glitch with the warrant. Milton lodged a harassment complaint when we failed to find evidence at his home. We'll get it, but it's going to take a little more time."

Adam felt the burning start in his chest and spread through his body as the familiar blanket of anger spread over him. "By then, Milton could leave, someone could tip them off, Bella could be taken elsewhere or used as bait for one of those pit bulls. I can't wait."

"Adam," her voice was soft and feminine, a sign she was trying to reason with him and didn't think anger would help the situation.

This wasn't the first time they'd been on a stake out or gone into a dangerous situation together. Adam knew the woman would use whatever weapon got the job done and that voice of hers affected a man. But, he wasn't fooled.

"Don't say it."

She frowned, but her lips remained soft, sadness pulling down at the corners. "They've had her for hours. She's a liability. She ties them to you and they think you're dead. You have to prepare yourself."

Looking out the windshield at the dancing branches playing hide-and-seek with the sun and shadows Adam contemplated what more to say to her. He'd unloaded a lot of difficult information for her to accept and to her credit, she was dealing with it better than he'd hoped. She was a rock. But, filtering additional information that she might find hard to believe was best for them both.

"She's still alive," he told her. What he couldn't say caught in his throat, held in check by his common sense, but sat there like hot lava in his gut. "You have to trust me."

"What's the plan?" she asked.

"Leave the car here for now. Sneak into the compound, locate Bella, rescue her, bring her back here and wait for the cavalry to arrive. Try to stay low profile if we can, face the consequences if we can't. But, if things go bad you come back to the vehicle and drive up the road into their compound."

"Make it look like we weren't here trespassing, spying and premeditating?"

"If we can extract Bella without alerting anyone that's the ideal. But, if that doesn't work out, we need to look like we simply arrived too early as we waited for a warrant we were sure is coming. We saw our guy and some drugs, and what else could we do?"

"So, my assignment, if things go wrong, isn't to watch your back, it's to cut and run?" She leaned back against her door to better face him.

"It's to ensure we do what we can to keep our jobs, and preserve our evidence."

Staring at him, she looked unconvinced, but she turned back, drew her pistol from her shoulder holster and checked it. She leaned across him, opened the glove box and took out extra ammo.

"You know," she opened the door, but turned back to ensure she looked him in the eye. "It's never about who we take down. It's about who we save. Every criminal we put into prison saves someone. Just because we never see it, doesn't make it less true. So before you harm anyone, you ask yourself, 'Is this about revenge? Retribution? Pride? Power?' It can never be about those things, Adam. And as long as everything we do is about saving people, I can swallow most any bullshit you throw at me. You understand?"

Wind blew in the opened kissing her wet skin and bringing strawberries and cream to remind him that this woman, tough as she was, had more compassion and courage than any woman he'd ever met. The stir in his chest told him he'd not shut off his emotions at all, regardless of his half-hearted effort. He was proud of her. Proud she was his partner.

"I understand."

# Chapter 8

BELLA WATCHED THE WATER run pink with her blood as it swirled and ran down the drain. She stood, allowing Cam to run his hands over her fur, shampooing away the blood and dirt from last night's encounter. Some of the blood was hers, but most of it was Adam's.

Glancing at the closed door of the bathroom she grunted as Cam's rough hand ran over a still-mending rib. She'd decided to act like all the other dogs there and pretend she just wanted to be loved by some human. Bile rose in her throat at the thought of pretending to be so gullible. But, her best shot at getting out and bringing Adam back to save the others was to bide her time until Cam fell asleep and slip out undetected. She was still hurt, and running while Cam could see her, perhaps shoot her, would only slow her down more. Max didn't have that kind of time.

Cam reeked of marijuana and Bella knew from previous encounters with humans who consumed the plant that it slowed them down, caused them to relax, eat and sleep. Watching him, adrenalin raced through her like lightning. His lids kept closing, eyes slightly rolling back in his head, movements slowing. She barked, needing him to hurry, then wagged her tail inviting him to feel as though she wanted to play.

"Okay girl. We're almost done." He shut off the water and turned to grab a towel. Lifting her out of the bath and setting her on the floor he began to rub her dry. He pushed hard enough on her rib to elicit a yelp. "Yeah, you took quite a beating last night." He cocked his head to the side and frowned, then dropped the towel to run his fingers through her fur. "Keeper said he cut you, but I think all that blood belonged to your owner. Keeper's an idiot, right girl?" He smiled.

Bella obliged by barking, tail wagging and doing her best to look happy.

Patting her head, he began drying her off, but was gentler about it.

"I looked you up on the internet," he told her in a soothing voice. "You're a Harlequin MinPin. Kind of rare to find a merle colored MinPin. I'd keep you if I could. But, JC has plans for you." He finished, threw the towel aside and pet her a moment longer.

Picking Bella up, he walked her back to her crate. He closed the door, but didn't lock it. Looking in at her he smiled. "It's a shame we have to kill you. I'll get you a treat. Something special." He looked over to Max's crate. "You too, Max." The sound of Max's tail hitting the side of the crate caused Cam's smile to broaden. "I'll be right back."

He shut the door behind him and several minutes went by. Bella got her treat. Just not the one he promised. The volume on the television went down and she could hear him snoring in the living room.

Bella pushed her paw between the bars and began batting at the latch.

# CHAPTER 9

K EEPER'S EYES BULGED AND tiny blood vessels began to pop. A large vein on his forehead stood out against the red and purple of his face.

"He can't answer you if you're choking the life out of him," Rebecca whispered and punched Adam in the shoulder, more to move him than hurt him. He didn't budge.

Adam released the man, but kept his gun trained on the pulsing vein dead center of the man's forehead. Keeper's deep intake of breath and subsequent coughing brought Rebecca back to the window of the trailer, looking out to make sure none of the other men were going to interrupt them.

Keeper staggered back grasping at his throat as though to protect it. His eyes still bulged from their sockets, but not because he was still choking.

"We killed you!" The man's words were a haggard whisper. "I saw you die."

Adam knew his expression was devoid of emotion. He knew how menacing he looked. He knew he could put his gun away and the man would still fear for his life.

"I don't die so easy." Adam stepped closer and Keeper backed up until he hit the wall. "But, I bet if I kill you, you'll stay dead."

Keeper slid down the wall, his legs no longer able to

hold his weight, and his bladder no longer in his control. "Please don't kill me. Please. I'll give you anything you want." He coughed and began crying.

"Tell me where my dog is," Adam demanded. Adam felt nothing and let that fact settle in his eyes as he stared at Keeper. "And if you tell anyone you saw us, I'll tell them you tried to kill me. Or," Adam lowered his voice as he crouched down to be face to face with man, "I'll say nothing and come for you myself."

Keeper began to sob hysterically. "I don't got the dog. I swear I don't. I swear!"

"I didn't ask if you have my dog, I asked you to tell me where she is."

"JC wanted her fixed up to fight, so Cam took her home. He's the dog medic. She's at his house." Keeper spoke so quickly the words slurred and ran together.

"And just where is that?" Adam felt his patience slipping and the urge for violence grew hot in his gut.

"It's on the far edge of the property. I can draw you a map." His voice became high pitched and the crying began again in earnest.

"We can't leave him here like that," Rebecca said, then quickly moved away from the window. "Someone's coming. Warren. It's your guy Warren." She immediately took up position beside the door, her gun pulled.

"Keep your mouth shut," Adam told Keeper and then stood to face the door.

Warren walked in, his attention intent on a text. He shut the door without a backward glance and had taken a step when Rebecca moved, putting the gun to the side of Warren's neck, causing the man to freeze like a statue.

"Be still, be quiet, cooperate," Rebecca said, taking the man's phone from his hands. "It's the best recipe for not getting shot today."

Keeper moved and Warren's attention shifted to where

Adam stood. Warren took a quick step back, nearly tripping when he ran into Rebecca. Rebecca pushed him away from her, but never lowered her gun.

"Shit!" Warren whispered. "Shit!" His voice got louder and Rebecca put the muzzle of the gun back to his neck.

"Let's keep it quiet," she warned.

He stepped back again, allowing Rebecca's gun to push into his flesh. It was as though he couldn't help himself.

"You're dead," Warren said, his voice trembling.

"I get that a lot," Adam answered. "So, were you the one to put the spikes in my head? Cause, you have to know, that really hurt. And it pissed me off."

Warren tried to back up again, but this time Rebecca shoved him. As the man righted himself a dark stain blossomed at his crotch and urine soaked his pants, some of it spilling into the floor.

"Jesus," Rebecca looked at the expanding puddle, then over at the quivering and equally messy Keeper. "Do you get *that* a lot?"

The urine odor quickly rode the heavy humidity and filled spread through the trailer. Adam grimaced. "It's not an unfamiliar event, no."

Rebecca leaned away from Warren who seemed glued in place. Reaching in her pocket she brought out her cell phone and looked at the screen. "We're a go."

Adam nodded. "You go back for the car and do the official thing. I'll just talk to these two about the error of their ways, and the exact location of my dog until you return."

"Don't leave us, lady," Warren begged. "This here thing is some kind of zombie."

Rebecca glanced at Adam, a smile flashed there for a moment then was gone. "Warren, that's not very P.C. of you." She checked outside, nodded to Adam and left.

From the window he saw her slink around the corner.

She'd be back in less than fifteen minutes. They'd counted five guys on the property, some of them moving dogs, putting them on treadmills, tethering them on a line for exercise. That included Keeper and Warren.

"While I'm out gathering your friends, the two of you can draw straws for who's coming with me to get my dog." He pulled out his handcuffs. "And guys? That was my conscience that just walked out that door. Don't do anything you'll regret while I'm gone. She'll be pissed as hell if she gets back and I've torn your arms off to beat you to death with."

# Chapter 10

ELLA LANDED ON HER feet, the pain in her side flaring for a moment, but she kept quiet. The other dogs quickly came forward, a few growing excited, whining, but none barked. Standing in front of Max's crate her heart felt a sharp pain that radiated through her small body. Unless they took action right away he wouldn't live much longer. The only consolation was that these bastards wouldn't get one more fight out of him as they'd hoped.

Slowly, she approached him. He smelled of medicine and blood, urine and infection. From her crate she was only able to see two thirds of his face, so when he turned his head to watch her approach she froze, alarm causing her to whine, sadness consuming her. A large part of his cheek was ravaged. A few stitches held it in place, but it was swollen and red. He'd have been a beautiful creature had he not been so savagely attacked.

She knew this was not the life he'd chosen for himself. Dogs didn't get to choose. Most dogs anyway. They'd clipped his ears, likely so they'd not be targets during the fights. He was covered in scars. Bella wished Max could understand her. She wished she knew more about being a normal dog. Those days were long behind her and only instinct and vague memories helped her now as she scooted on her belly, inching toward him.

A low growl echoed within Max's crate and she stopped. Propping her head on her front paws she rested. Max was confined, injured and saw other dogs as threats. It wasn't going to be easy to release him. After considering his current condition she wasn't sure it was a good idea to let him out. How far could he get? Would he even try to leave? Bella's heart fell and she sighed.

She needed Adam. And she needed to get Cam to open the door so she could escape. The only way to save Max at this point was to be quick, and get help.

She stood and Max tried to stand, but he gave up. He didn't growl, but his eyes were shiny and alert now. Walking over to the metal trash can Bella pushed it over and rolled it to the stool near the makeshift exam table Cam had left down earlier. The can banged against the stool and some of the dogs began to bark. She moved it back and pushed it again and the sound caused more dogs to bark. By the sixth time she had everyone riled and barking and footsteps sounded just outside the door.

Her ears twitched, moving to take in the sound outside the door. The click of the door handle being turned, the hinges moving, Bella positioned herself low and just out of sight. Cam threw the door open and she rushed him, moving between his legs before he could react.

"Damn dog!"

Cam's voice followed her. She knew not to waste precious time looking back. Picking up as much speed as she could, ignoring the pain throbbing in her side, she reached the living room and launched herself into the air hitting the box fan in the window with all her might. The fan crashed backward and out onto the front porch. She was free in an instant rushing toward the dirt road as fast as her legs could carry her when the shot rang out, pain seared through her body and she dropped like a stone to the ground.

# Chapter 11

ADAM STOOD IN THE center of the compound watching Rebecca's approach. The men next to him were all on their asses, bleeding, and bruised but otherwise still breathing. He could see her scrunch her face, purse her lips and evil-eye him before the car came to a full stop.

Rebecca got out shaking her head and joined him. "Patience is not one of your virtues," she said, her voice devoid of humor.

"They chose not to come peacefully," Adam informed her. "And nobody died."

"And that's how we're defining a 'win' these days?"

Adam shrugged.

"And the piss-twins?" She cut her eyes to the trailer that held Keeper and Warren.

"Handcuffed to each other, but otherwise unharmed. I put a bow on these guys for you and now I need to find Bella."

"I heard from headquarters. We should have backup here any minute. They've called an animal rescue team to come get these poor dogs. Their days of fighting are over."

Adam nodded. "These guys aren't going anywhere. Can I leave you to it?"

"Yeah, I'll stay here and wait, but let me know where you're going so I can back you up, just in case."

Adam looked at the three men sitting on the ground.

"Don't go anywhere."

They glared, but said nothing. Adam and Rebecca turned to head back to the trailer, Rebecca gesturing at her eyes with her right hand, then pointing to them making sure they understood she'd be watching them.

They left the front door open, not fully trusting the men to be good for their word. Rebecca stood just inside the doorframe. Warren and Keeper came to attention when the door opened, standing to face them, thrusting a piece of paper toward Adam.

"Here's a map," Keeper said, his hands shaking as Adam took the drawing. "Takes maybe twenty minutes to get there from here. Easy route. Can't miss it."

As Adam studied the drawing a loud chirping interrupted him. Keeper looked over to the cell phone on the coffee table as it vibrated with each ring. Adam walked over, picked it up and showed Keeper the display with Cam's name on it. Handing it to Keeper he nodded and Keeper answered.

Rebecca walked over, took the phone and hit the speaker button, putting her finger to her lips in warning.

Keeper swallowed hard before talking. "What is it?"

"Man, I'm screwed. Max isn't going to make it long enough for another fight. You may as well just stay there. JC is going to be pissed. Max won't make it and I had to shoot that Marshal's dog. I am never going to hear the end of it."

Keeper's eyes filled with tears and his voice sounded like a choir boy singing soprano when he answered. "What! You killed the Marshal's dog? Are you crazy? Are you sure it's dead? Oh my God. What have you done?"

"Jesus, Keeper, you were ready to kill her when we captured her."

"You're sure she's dead?" Keeper asked again, this time his voice giving way to fear, quivering.

"I'm sure she's dead. Looks like I got her heart. It's too hot to build a fire in the pit right now, but when the sun sets I'll get rid of the body."

Adam checked the time, shook his head at Keeper and pointed to the phone.

"No!" Keeper shouted. He cleared his throat in a visible effort to control himself. "I mean, don't do anything until I hear from JC. Okay?"

There was a long pause, but then Cam answered. "Because you think JC wants to keep a dead dog? Are you high?"

Keeper forced out an abrupt laugh that sounded more like he was choking on glass. "I might be high. You know me. But, JC was particular about that dog. I'm just lookin' out for you. Bad enough about Max."

Another pause, just long enough Adam felt cold fingers run up his spine.

"I'll just call JC," Cam answered. "You better sober up before he gets there."

The phone disconnected and Keeper started crying again. Rebecca carefully removed the phone from his trembling hands.

"Adam," she spoke softly, calm. "I am so sorry. I know you want to do right by her and bury her yourself. The plan is still to go and get her. We have time."

It took him a moment to really see her. Thoughts of Bella's body being turned to ash before she could heal enough to escape caused his heart to flex with pain and terror. As he focused and his mind began to comprehend his environment the look in her eyes brought back to the moment. The beautiful blue shined as though the wetness in them caught the light that streamed in from the open door. But, something else lived there, something he knew all too well because he'd seen it more times than he cared to imagine; fear. Reality continued to pour in and the weight of a warm body against his pushed him the rest of the way into the moment.

He released Keeper from his grasp as he lowered the knife he couldn't recall retrieving from the inside of his coat. The man collapsed, terrified but unharmed, to the floor. Those seconds had ticked by and he was the monster, with the instinct of the killer he'd been created to be. Humanity, carefully cultivated and added to his personal skillset, fell away and he stumbled like a misstep in an intricate dance. There inside those seconds Marshal Rebecca Hughes saw him. He could see it reflected in the fear in her eyes. She truly saw him. And in those seconds it was obvious that she knew what he had tried to convince her of since this morning; he is a monster greater than the myth ever was.

"Put the knife away, Adam," she instructed, the soft, caring voice careful in tone.

Looking down at the knife he blinked hard and shook his head. Most of the vertigo from earlier was gone, but it took a moment for his eyes to see clearly. He tucked the knife away and stepped back from Keeper.

The sound of tires, car engines turning off and slamming doors brought Adam's attention to the open door. Two sedans, company issue, pulled up and four marshals approached. Two ran to the men tied up outside and the others came to the open door.

"Vasquez," Rebecca nodded in greeting to first the female marshal, then the male, "Gustov."

"Jesus, Hughes it smells like piss in here," Elena Vasquez was short, compact and nearly forty. Her long, dark hair pulled back in a braid highlighted a high forehead and nearly-black eyes. Black eyes that always seemed to take in every little detail.

Adam thought that was likely the reason she didn't like him. She asked too many questions, like she didn't think he quite added up.

"I'm sure I'm going to regret asking this," William "Will" Gustov said as he walked in and stood next to Rebecca, "But, what the hell's going on here? Why is everyone pissing themselves?" The last part was directed at Adam.

Adam stared blankly at his colleagues as he asked, "Anyone here feel their rights have been violated and want to lodge a complaint?"

Both Warren and Keeper answer "No."

Rebecca bit at the corner of her lip before turning to Vasquez. "Listen, we really need you and Gustov to handle these guys and wait for the animal rescue people to arrive. Someone took Adam's dog and we need to go get her. She was shot."

"What? Someone shot Bella?" Vasquez stepped inside, the hardness around her eyes melting away to concern. Looking at Keeper and Warren the hardness returned. "Where the hell is she?"

Adam felt his control beginning to slip, the need to get to Bella making it harder to pretend he was able to deal with the situation like a normal human being. "Maybe she's shot, maybe not, but someone has her and I'm leaving to get her."

From his peripheral vision he noted the quizzical look on Rebecca's face. There was no time to talk it out.

"We've got this," Vasquez assured him. "Go get Bella."

"Hey," Gustov interjected. "This entire property is included in the warrant. If you leave the property, you're not covered."

Adam nodded.

"I'm going with you," Rebecca said and was walking out the door before he could respond.

As they left the compound, following the map Keeper and Warren had gave them, Rebecca sped up.

"I knew Vasquez was sweet on that dog," she said. A

few moments passed and she pulled in a long breath. "I know you're holding out hope, Adam, but you need to get yourself under control and be prepared."

"Just drive."

To her credit she let it go and added more speed.

The humidity kept the dust from rising too high around them, but couldn't keep the cloud of it from flying in their wake. The trees grew denser, the sun throwing thin lines of light in a valiant effort to reach the road as branches clothed in thick leaves reached out to entwine overhead giving the last mile of their trip a canopy, enclosing them in a tunnel created by nature.

Adam's heart beat faster the closer they got to the place where the man, Cam, had Bella. The place where Cam intended to set her on fire. The mage who gave Bella to Adam, as payment for saving the man's daughter, said Bella was immortal. But, immortality was like magic; it existed until someone figured out how it worked and how to overcome it.

The tunnel grew wider until it opened up into a big field. In the center of the field were two buildings and an old pickup. The storage building looked like it was held up by wishful thinking and sheer will. The doublewide trailer sat on gray cinderblocks, rust decorated the seams of metal that popped out of place here and there. A large blue tarp covered the roof at one end, bricks holding it place so it wouldn't fly away. Adam took it all in, but it was the rising gray smoke behind the trailer that caused his mouth to go dry.

"Shit," Rebecca voiced the same concern Adam was feeling. "JC must have told him to take care of it right away." She stopped the car. "You go around to the right, I'll go left."

He was out, heading right, gun pulled. His size always made people think he would be slow, which was in his favor. He was fast. Really fast. As he rounded the trailer his brain absorbed all the information at once.

Cam stood in front of a fire pit, flames high in the air, the scent of kerosene riding the wind. At the man's feet was a small black and gray body, wet with the same kerosene that had helped get the fire started. Bella lay motionless, unable to stop what was about to happen to her. The one creature in all the world that loved him was being picked up by the scruff of her neck to be tossed into the flames. And as fast as he was, he wouldn't make it in time to stop it.

Crying out in despair he launched his body toward Cam as the man pulled his arm back to throw Bella's body, then a shot rang out, echoing in Adam's ears, followed by Cam's scream. Blood splattered Adam's face, but he was able to catch Bella as Cam dropped her. Adam rolled away from the open flames, Bella's body cradled against his chest.

He moved to ensure his weight wouldn't crush her. She was covered in blood and he looked for the entry point. The bullet had gone through her, but was already beginning to heal. The fumes of the kerosene caused his eyes to water and he stood, her limp body in his arms. A water hose was feet away and he turned it on, washing the kerosene off of her, making sure it wasn't in her eyes, nose or mouth where it might burn.

"Bella?" He whispered to her as though she might be sleeping. "Bella, I'm here." He heard the tap, tap, tap against his coat before he felt it; her tail. He closed his eyes, willing away the lump in his throat and trying to force his heart too slow. The burning behind his eyes gave a slight haze to his vision as he saw her eyes open. "You're going to be okay. I've got you." Gathering her close he stood, cradling her, petting her head as gently as he could.

Looking to where Cam had been standing he saw

Rebecca helping the man up, checking out his bleeding wrist. She pushed the guy forward despite his cries of pain. Their eyes met and hers grew round with surprise.

"She's alive?"

He smiled. "Yes."

"We need to call an ambulance for this asshole," she said as she continued walking back in the direction in which she'd come. "And get the animal rescue over here, too. I can hear dogs barking inside."

Adam followed her inside, holding a now-animated Bella who licked his face and neck with enthusiasm. Once inside she barked and he sat her down. She stumbled, but backed away when Adam tried to pick her up again.

Rebecca guided Cam to the couch, but he screamed as though she was stabbing him. Once he sat down his eyes landed on Bella and he gasped.

"There is no way that dog is alive," he said. "I shot her. Hit her heart. That can't be the same dog."

"Something tells me you're not quite the shot you think," Rebecca answered, pointing to all the drugs on the coffee table.

Bella barked again, swaying as though she were drunk, but moving down the hallway to a door at the end. Adam followed. The barking grew louder and he realized she wanted him to know about the other dogs. He opened the door and Bella went straight to one crate in particular, whining as she sat in front of it.

Crouching down Adam looked inside. "Rebecca," he yelled. "Tell those animal rescue people we need medical attention immediately. They need to get here fast."

Bella collapsed in front of the dog's kennel and Adam reached out to soothe her, rubbing her ear slowly between his thumb and index finger. "We'll get him some help, girl. It's going to be okay."

# Chapter 12

NIGHT HAD COME AND brought a million stars. The moon was full giving even the shadows a silvery glow. Adam walked out onto his front porch and breathed in the cool, clean air. The large picture window gave its own golden illumination by way of a path across the porch swing and into the gravel driveway and over the hood of Rebecca's car.

"One of those for me?" she asked, indicating the two beer bottles in his hand.

He handed her one and sat on the bench across from the swing where she'd tucked her legs beneath her, looking comfortable. She took a long pull of the cold beer, sat it down on the ground and moved so she could pull a box from off the ground at the side of the swing. She smiled as she handed it to him and then sat back down and picked up her beer.

Bella rushed out of the dog door and jumped up next to Adam. The light didn't quite reach them on the bench and Adam was comfortable with the shadows. Sitting the box on his lap he rubbed Bella's fur in long strokes down her back, then pet her head softly and picked the box up once more.

"Open it," Rebecca encouraged.

He removed the lid and pulled out the black Stetson.

"Thank you."

"This time try to take better care with it," she teased.

He put it on his head and wondered how she'd guessed the right size. As a very large man, it wasn't always easy to find things that fit him. But, this fit perfectly.

Sitting forward, taking a drink, he cleared his throat. "Max is doing better?"

"Yes, it's going to take some time for him to fully recover, but eventually he will. I think Vasquez may take him."

"And the other dogs?"

"They get tested to see if they can be rehabilitated. There are some rescues willing to take them in and work with them. There were over one hundred dogs, so it's a pretty big and time-intensive endeavor. But, already they have better prospects than they had before."

She brought her leg out and sat it on the ground to gently push herself back and forth in the swing. The rhythm slow and gentle. Crickets sang, nature rising up in a chorus of harmony.

Adam hated to break the easy silence, but it had been a week since they'd saved Bella and shut down the dog fighting ring and neither of them had talked much about everything that had happened. Rebecca had started making him go out after work and hang with some of the other marshals. Her observation that he needed to work on his social skills was as irritating as it was true, but he relented and, in the end, was glad.

He invited her over for dinner to thank her and to gauge how she was dealing with everything he'd told her about himself.

"I need to ask you something," he said and wondered what it meant when she stopped rocking and took a deep drink of her beer.

"Like what?"

"You thought Bella was dead when that guy started

to toss her into the fire. But, you shot him, knowing you could lose your job, a career you love, so he would drop her body. Some people wouldn't have done that for a living dog. You did it when you thought she was dead. Why?"

She looked out into the forest, then up at the stars before looking back at him. Shrugging, she said, "Something about how you love her." She paused as though carefully considering her words. "It doesn't matter that she's a dog. Love like that matters. It saves people. Their souls, you know? To lose her like that, in a fire, right in front of you, I was afraid of what that might do to you. In the end it wasn't about stopping him. It was about saving you."

His heart absorbed the warmth of her words and her kindness.

"You don't really know me, Rebecca," he said, knowing it was only right to warn her. He knew what she'd seen when he nearly killed Keeper. She'd seen the murderous creature that lived somewhere inside him. "You can't know if I'm worth saving."

"Call it a hunch," she said and started rocking the swing once more. "And in the end I was right about you."

"How so?"

"I saw the look on your face when he was about to toss her into the fire. Rage. Despair. Pain. But, when he dropped her you didn't attack him. Most people can't turn emotions like that off instantaneously. You didn't go for him. Instead, you went for her. You were doing the same thing I was. You weren't looking at stopping him. You were looking at saving her."

He sat back, thinking and his hand fell naturally to petting Bella. She rested her head on crossed paws and looked content.

Texas was growing on him. He enjoyed being a marshal. And despite his many social obstacles, he was making friends. He leaned back and stretched his long legs out in front of him, crossing them at his ankles. He pulled the Stetson down over his eyes, ran his hand over Bella's soft fur and enjoyed the peaceful quiet of nature's music and the sound of the rocking porch swing.

## The End

# Note About Dog Fighting

DOG FIGHTING IS CRUEL and illegal, but lucrative, so it continues to happen all over the world.

This cruel event if often seen by children and accompanies other illegal activity.

You can search online for The Humane Society's tip line to report dog fighting. They even have a program where you can be paid reward money.

If you know of a dog fight, dog fighting ring, or suspect dog fighting you can call your local law enforcement and report it. Please do speak up. These poor animals have no voice but yours.

# Sample Chapter of Upcoming Releases

**C**IRCLE OF **S**EVEN BEGINS an urban fantasy series about a covert group of leaders. Each is a king of his people and they work together to govern the supernatural in a modern world.

In Circle of Seven the King of Immortals has gone mad and an ancient artifact has been stolen. Raven is hired to find the artifact, but she's not the only one after it. Rohan, once the leader of his people, now exiled, wants the Immortal Sword returned to him. Espionage, hostile takeovers and political intrigue are high stakes on an all-new level.

**S**HADOWS **A**CROSS THE **M**OON - Near-future San Francisco loses power as a mysterious fog rolls in carrying with it death and destruction by way of cyborgs and a deadly terrorist bio-agent.

Grace Sullivan is an indentured servant with nothing to lose, thrown together with rock star and entrepreneur Thomas Dane when the city becomes a deadly prison, the site of a secret government terrorist attack that will kill all living things in the city.

Time is running out for Grace on every level as she finds courage to fight against the training of her class to save those left behind in the darkened city while she fights the overpowering attraction to the man she blames for the fall of humanity.

# CIRCLE OF SEVEN

## CHAPTER 1

THE NIGHT HADN'T GONE as planned. Being kidnapped, drugged, shot and waking up in a vampire's bed was never on the agenda. At least I'd escaped, the bullet hadn't hit anything vital, and the vampire was gorgeous. One girl's nightmare is another's good luck.

The intense throb in my head was ignored for the stabbing fire of pain in my shoulder. Waking to pain heightened the senses and one's need for self-preservation.

The large canopy bed was soft and slick with black satin sheets, warmth from a nearby fireplace wasn't making me any warmer, it was dark, and I was nude. Pulling the sheets with me, I pushed my back up against the cold headboard while scanning the room. The faint firelight cast dancing shadows on three doors. One had to be an exit. There was an armoire across from me, directly in front of the bed, and two chairs faced the front of the fireplace. Someone sat in the chair to the left, staring toward the fire. It was Daniel Forester, sitting still as a statue. At least he was trying to warm that cold, vampire's body of his with the fireplace and not me. A vague memory itched in my brain and scratching at it brought about the memory of his body next to mine. Varied levels of consciousness throughout my stay here left reality at the mercy of untrustworthy dreams.

"Raven Peterson," the voice was softer than the sheets, "You've been out for two days." A slow turn of the head and a sweeping gaze made me bristle. Mentally, I prepared myself to fight off any compulsion, but it never came.

"Two days?" That rolled around in my mind for a minute. Where was my stuff? Where was I? And most importantly, where was my 9 mm semi-automatic?

The flicker of light in shadow brought my attention to the oncoming vampire. He hadn't made a sound. I hate that.

He stood next to the bed half in shadow, half in firelight. His silence was unnerving. Was I supposed to do something?

"Where are my weapons?" My eyes wanted to go anywhere but to his.

His feet made no sound on the carpet as he walked to the armoire and pulled something off the top of it.

He handed me my Derringer, my 9 mm, and a four-inch stainless steel blade that fit in a sheath at my thigh. He sat them next to the bed on a side table that had escaped my notice. The drugs, compliments of my kidnappers, were still affecting my abilities.

The weapons were within reach and that made me more comfortable. Would it be considered rude to put the Derringer under my pillow while he stood there?

"What happened?"

"We escaped. You took a bullet in your shoulder and hit your head when you fell. Now you are here, at my home." He paused and added, "You've healed surprisingly fast."

Curious about my ability to heal, but unwilling to ask about it outright, Daniel left the last as a statement. The comment hung in the air unanswered. It's good to keep someone guessing, especially if you are naked and they are not.

Shaking my head to clear the cobwebs in my throbbing brain had not been a good idea. The shadow of a memory faded in and out. It was enough to know there was something I should remember, but not enough to actually remember it. The figure of a tall man, dark and muscular, came to me. His eyes were gray and unusual. Daniel moved, and the memory shattered into nothingness.

"Was there someone else there who helped us escape?" I felt him in my memory. "Where is he now?"

"If there was, I didn't see him," Daniel replied. Something in his voice said "lie", but it was buried deep beneath a layer of seduction. "The only man we should be concerned with now is Gabriel Kearney."

That bastard Gabriel did this. But why? Why hire me to look at an ancient sword and then kidnap me? This was supposed to be a sweetheart gig. Research, authenticate, ensure the thing wasn't cursed, and prep it for a safe journey to the highest bidder. The money was great, and desperately needed. Too good to be true…always gets Raven in trouble.

My gaze drifted about the room as memories came forward in waves. Mr. Forrester had been much kinder to me than I had been to him. Dungeon etiquette always escaped me. But, Mr. Forrester apparently knew all kinds of etiquette. Immaculate room for an unexpected guest, no hanky panky with the unconscious girl, and weapons at the bedside. Great guy. He seemed trustworthy but was entirely too gorgeous with that long blonde hair and perfect body. It would be a shame to have to kill him.

"I know why I was at Kearney's place." The statement was an invitation to Daniel to share more information.

"I had planned on stealing the sword," he said without out a hint of remorse. "It is very valuable. Unfortunately, I was captured"

"Well, I was an invited guest," I wondered if Daniel's choice to remain where he was had to do with wanting the heat from the fire or not wanting to spook me. He was being careful. He wanted something. I needed to get out of here.

"Looks like my clothes are missing."

"Yes, I fear your shirt was ruined." An elaborate gesture of his hand indicated there was nothing else he could have done. He walked to the armoire and retrieved a shirt. "Blood can always be cleaned, but bullet holes are forever."

The shirt was too big, but it was a soft material that felt cool as my fingers caressed it. As I wondered what it would feel like on my skin, I took inventory of my body.

Someone had cleaned me up, and only a small scar was left where the bullet hole had been. That would be gone in a few days too. Healing quickly was nothing to a vampire, but for a human it was impressive. So, we knew a little something about each other now. He knew I healed quickly, and I knew from our great escape, he was a vampire. We were even, and that seemed fair to me. One rule I had; okay I had a few rules, but this one was a big one; you never let someone know what your powers are. I couldn't hide the healing, but there were far more interesting things Mr. Forrester would not get to know.

"You were invited?" Daniel encouraged me to continue.

"I was hired to authenticate the sword. Easy gig. Big money," I told him.

"Easy, and big, money didn't tip you off? What kind of detective are you?"

"I didn't say I was a detective." Of course, he would've gone through my wallet.

"I know who you are, Raven. I just don't know *what* you are."

Daniel had not moved. He stared at me, seemingly waiting for something. For an instant, I had a wild thought about how soft his hair looked. Compulsion? Effects of the drugs? The hit on the head?

He wore jeans and a black, long-sleeved, satin button up shirt. It was tucked in, and a black belt was hooked through the loops in his jeans. The first two buttons of his shirt were undone, revealing a hairless chest. He had no jewelry, and his hair was tied back. A couple of strands had come loose and hung in his face. They were long with a slight curl, falling beneath a strong jaw line. My gaze followed the curl up as far as his eyes, but the blue was unnatural and brought me back to my senses. My mind drifted between real and fantasy; between survival and desire.

"I will pay you whatever Gabriel Kearney promised if you find that sword. Twice that amount if you bring it to me. Are you interested?" He was asking and being very polite. His patience was that of a predator.

"I don't work for vampires."

"I *am* a vampire." He was straight forward, and I could respect that. "And what are you?"

After years of owning a paranormal detective agency, you saw enough to know when even a vampire was hiding something.

"Raven," he stepped closer and his voice dropped an octave. "Gabriel Kearney is a very evil man. A dangerous man. Clearly, I cannot do this alone. But we worked very well together to escape him. To outsmart him." When I said nothing he continued. "Vampire status notwithstanding, I am honest, and I can pay half up front." His smile showed unearthly white teeth. The tone of his voice had the cadence of a lullaby. It left me feeling warm and sleepy. Looking at him was a mistake. Eyes as blue as sapphires sparkled with intensity.

The myth was that a vampire didn't cast a reflection. I knew that to be wrong. That fact had saved my life once. Mirrors weren't holy objects or supernatural. Maybe the myth about vampires casting no reflection came from that saying, "the eyes are the mirrors of the soul." In that case, it was true. Vampires often cast no reflection of themselves there at all.

"You're a beautiful woman, Raven," he said as he took another step closer to the bed. "Your eyes are like mine. Sapphires."

Panic fought to flow through my veins. Could he read minds? I wanted to blank my mind out just in case. But it only helped create that sense of dizzying surrender to the need for peaceful rest…or sex.

Was this place far from San Francisco? How long would it take to get home? Would Aden and Tory be looking for me? Now I needed to fill my mind with anything but the thought of Daniel's hard body.

There had been no bells and whistles. Compulsion usually had a signature feel to it. There had been no bells and whistles with Gabriel Kearney either. There wasn't a lot on the man, but the story he gave checked out when we researched it. Tory O'Malley, a psychic on staff and a damned good detective, wanted me to have back up and weapons since we barely knew Gabriel Kearney. She said it wasn't a premonition, just her normal paranoia. I should've listened to her.

Aden Tascher, another detective, researched the alleged curse. Aden happened to be a witch, something that came in handy with my chosen clientele. That was as normal as it got at my agency.

A limo ride, a long wait, a proper English butler. That should have tipped me off. It was all too perfect. The drugs had to be in the ice cubes. The drugs were potent enough to cause my vision to blur less than a minute after the first drink. Less than two minutes and there was nothing to see but darkness.

That's when I woke to find myself slick with dungeon goop and the knowledge that someone was none too gentle with throwing me into the cell. Perhaps they thought my cellmate would save them the trouble of killing me, but instead we joined forces and busted out. The only missing piece to this was the man in the shadows who somehow helped us. The one Daniel denied was there.

The movement of the bed drew me out of my own thoughts. Daniel was climbing into bed, naked.

# Shadows Across the Moon

## Chapter 1

Looking down on the casket Grace Sullivan imagined herself inside. Not that she wanted to be dead, but the woman inside had been loved by many, celebrated for her skill with a violin. That woman had touched people's hearts, filled their souls with solace and peace through her music and those people stood around the casket crying, some sobbing, all of them remembering someone that mattered.

Grace loved music. She loved this woman's music even though it was often melancholy. Over the last few weeks Grace had listened to the sad music of the violin often. First she listened for peace, to calm her nerves after the blow she'd received recently regarding her own future. Then, she listened because the music and her own soul became kindred spirits, dancing through her mind, her heart, a desperate waltz.

So she came to the funeral, part out of curiosity, part out of respect and part because funerals had become an addiction for her and this one was going to be huge. No one would notice her, no strange stares from the family, no frowns from the funeral director. Most funerals were very small of course, but she knew this one would be well attended and she'd worked extra hours in order to get this time off to attend.

The people gathered around the coffin were mostly high society and she wondered if they would notice her cast off dress from three seasons ago, or the cheap shoes. In her experience, those people always noticed. It was cold out, the breeze coming in from the ocean, salting the air and cooling as it moved like a liquid blanket over the mourners. Grace adjusted her satchel and then hunkered deeper inside her long jacket, the only garment she had that was name brand and could pass for more than her servant's second hand wardrobe. It had been a gift from her employer just recently. He knew her situation and though he'd never shown a great deal of caring for her, he'd gone out and got her this gift. Pity gift maybe? That was the only explanation she could come up with. She tried not to be bitter, tried to remain respectful, continue going about her day as though she would live to see another year even though that wasn't going to happen.

"Maybe she was a servant for her?" Someone whispered and it carried the words across the casket, to the other side where Grace stood in the second row of people.

Looking up she saw the two women eyeing her like she was some anomaly. And, in a way she was. She knew that. She'd become hyper-attuned to any conversations that might have to do with her presence at a funeral. She had to. She didn't really belong here. She'd been asked to leave a funeral just last week because the family didn't know her, and because, apparently, the gentleman who had died had a wife who suspected any young woman was a mistress of her dead husband's. Mistresses had been prohibited from attending, but funerals were addictive to a lot of people, so funeral directors were like detectives, and bouncers all rolled into one.

Grace could see fog rolling in and slowly started to back away from the crowd. Getting caught in the fog, especially so close to sundown was enough to move her away from such an amazing event. She'd heard enough. Enough sobbing, enough crying, enough final words and remembrances, enough snide remarks hidden behind covered mouths to friends who probably went just to show off their travel skills and new clothes.

She walked toward the BART station, San Francisco's infamous transport system, with only one last glance back at the crowd. When her time came there would be no crowd. Indentured servants were cremated or their bodies donated to science. She already knew which would be her fate. They'd told her.

She sighed, drawing in the salt air, and drew her jacket tighter around her. She realized the first pangs of a headache and hoped it would pass. She'd lived to be well into her twenties. Her life was better than some. She'd be damned if she would spend her remaining time feeling sorry for herself. That wasn't why she attended funerals. Not just to imagine what her own death might be like. No, she'd been attending funerals since she was trained to use the BART system. She was more curious about other people's lives. It was like looking at a picture of someone you don't know and wondering what they were like, what their life was like, when the picture was taken. It had less to do with death and more to do with who someone affected the life and lives around them that Grace was interested in. There was more to it, she knew, but her addiction wasn't as macabre as some people might think.

As she stepped up onto the concrete just outside the station she was jarred out of inner musings by a jolt to her shoulder. The man, dressed in a dark suit, stumbled as he tried to jostle several items in his arms and rammed into Grace's shoulder. He didn't look at her, didn't apologize and continued to move as though the devil himself were behind him. Grace frowned, unsurprised at the man's behavior. Regardless of what they taught you in school, when you were live with people out in the open it was difficult to recall all of the rules of etiquette you were taught through school lessons. She shook her head, happy not to have been knocked down, and glanced around to ensure no one else was coming up behind her.

Her heart had skipped a beat when she'd first realized someone was that close to her, but she calmed herself, as she was trained to do under these circumstances, and chanted quietly in her head, "It doesn't matter now. It doesn't matter now." Words that gave her courage to deal with the unexpected actions of people. Courage was a little easier to come by when there was little to lose.

Grace stepped inside, away from death, just to plug in and meet it once again.

Chaos reigned. Over a million people were dead. Detroit, as the world once knew it, was gone.

Footage played on a television screen, which was located in Grace's head, behind her eyes. A slight glitch in the picture caused Grace to pull the 4-inch rod from a hole near the inside of her ear. Frowning at the new headset, she blew on the end of the metal rod, an old trick a teacher once showed her.

Being unplugged from her headset was uncomfortable. She'd noticed that some of the people at the funeral were plugged in the entire time, which was a breach of etiquette for such events, but no one really said anything. She had been craving it too, the headset, like most of America, but because she had ventured out into the city, into the unfamiliar, she kept herself unplugged until she was sure she didn't need to interact.

Though most people in San Francisco worked inside their homes, there was still life on the streets. People moved without acknowledging each other because they didn't know how to interact socially anymore. Sure, she was nervous to be out, but the thrill of it was an adventure.

One not often extended to an indentured servant.

Grace looked around the BART station. What was once a huge train station that carried thousands of commuters each day was nearly empty. The trains had been replaced by 2-person commuter pods. The need to commute replaced by a 4-inch rod that you could insert into your head to watch television, listen to radio, go to school, order online, whatever you wanted.

As she waited for the next pod to come, she inserted the rod and was plugged in.

It had been ten years since the fall of Detroit. Ten years to the day. And every station she watched only wanted to highlight those horrific scenes of dead bodies and fear.

A pod, across the platform, pulled up. Grace concentrated on the screen behind her eyes. She could see someone get out, but she preferred to concentrate on the television.

The fall of Detroit to a bioterrorist weapon, a weapon that was still unidentified by American scientists, seemed so far away from San Francisco. Once, Detroit had been one of the grossly overpopulated cities, but not anymore. The bio-weapon had killed all living things; flora, fauna, wildlife... People. The death toll was quickly forgotten by the nation's leaders. Or so it seemed, by the quick government take over of the land, and the re-population of New Detroit. But the people, the American people themselves, didn't forget.

It was too frightening to watch, so she skipped around to a channel that wasn't showing those terrible scenes.

*"Be in love ... be in lust ... be happy; Emotions in Motion can give you all you need."* The voice filled her head. *"Plug in to 1-800-Emotionchip or <u>www.emotionchip. com</u> and you can feel your way to the top."* The voice was replaced by another, softer voice. *"You must present your mating license to purchase love or lust chips."*

The Emotion Chip was the hottest selling thing on the market. For those who could afford such luxury. In the year 2095, they couldn't stop over-population, but using a chip to fall in love became serious business.

Thomas Dane, one of the worlds most wealthy, most influential, and most talented men had designed the Emotion Chip. In Grace's opinion that chip only caused a great rift between people and emotions, between socialization and hierarchy. If it weren't for the fact that the man could sing so beautifully, and that he had the most beautiful brown eyes, she wouldn't buy any of his inventions, records, or DVDs.

A blast of air, cold and unmerciful, ran up her coat and she shivered. It was a sign that the pod was coming. As the wind died down, she heard footsteps coming her way. She had hoped not to have to share the pod.

"Hold on!" His voice was sharp, but deep.

The white pod stopped, the door opened automatically to let her inside. She really didn't want to share the small space with a stranger. Her finger hovered over the HOLD button. Should she acknowledge the man or not?

She had been taught by her teachers to say little and understand her position in life. The government trained her to be subservient, but she had always found subtle ways to rebel. She had been fighting it since she was a child. The government took her at the tender age of four from parents who were guilty of having a child without a mating license. They installed a hook-up and she started school--sitting in a lonely, sterile room. She was to be forced into servitude until she could pay the fines of her illegal birth. *Sins of the father...*

She would not be ruled by a social handicap. Her finger depressed the button. It turned red. Her heart beat harder, faster, as she waited. She sought solace by concentrating on the television program.

The pod shuddered and dipped as its new occupant climbed in. Her finger moved from the button as she stared out the front of the vehicle.

Interest. Curiosity. She fought both inclinations as etiquette dictated. A dark figure in her peripheral vision. Even from the corner of her eye, she could see the man was large, muscular, tall. She chanced a quick flick of her eyes in his direction, trying not to move her head and give herself away. Something about him was familiar. She looked forward again and her heart sped up. He was older than her, but not by a lot. She could see his hands, large with long fingers, well-manicured, not rough, not worker's hands. Whether it was his confidence in moving about, being around someone else, or his masculine aura that sped her heart she was uncertain. Her awareness of him heightened and she wondered if she hadn't just made a huge mistake.

# About the Author:

SHEILA ENGLISH WAS BORN and raised in the Redwoods of California. Now, a Kentucky resident, she works each day in a life-sized Tardis where she writes novels, scripts and works at COS Productions as the CEO and a producer.

When not traveling, she lives at home with her family and seven dogs. She may have a dog addiction. She collects vintage typewriters, cameras and telephones as well as collecting dog décor. She is a huge Doctor Who fan and loves anything nerdy.

You can find out more at her website at
www.SheilaEnglish.com, or on social media
Twitter- @SheilaEnglish67 or @cosproductions
Facebook.com/booktrailers

You can also email her at Sheila.English@gmail.com

Made in the USA
Charleston, SC
15 October 2016